Praise for the

FIXIN' TO DIE (#1)

"Packed with clever plot twists, entertaining characters, and plenty of red herrings! *Fixin' To Die* is a rollicking, delightful, down-home mystery."

– Ann Charles,
USA Today Bestselling Author of the Deadwood Mystery Series

"Southern and side-splitting funny! *Fixin' To Die* has captivating characters, nosy neighbors, and is served up with a ghost and a side of murder."

– Duffy Brown,
Author of the Consignment Shop Mysteries

"This story offers up a small touch of paranormal activity that makes for a fun read...A definite "5-star," this is a great mystery that doesn't give up the culprit until the last few pages."

– *Suspense Magazine*

"Kappes captures the charm and quirky characters of small-town Kentucky in her new mystery...a charming, funny story with exaggerated characters. The dialect-filled quirky sayings and comments bring those characters to life."

– *Lesa's Book Critiques*

"A Southern-fried mystery with a twist that'll leave you positively breathless."

– Susan M. Boyer,
USA Today Bestselling Author of *Lowcountry Book Club*

SOUTHERN
FRIED

**The Kenni Lowry Mystery Series
by Tonya Kappes**

SOUTHERN FRIED

A KENNI LOWRY MYSTERY

TONYA KAPPES

HENERY PRESS

SOUTHERN FRIED
A Kenni Lowry Mystery
Part of the Henery Press Mystery Collection

First Edition | April 2017

Henery Press, LLC
www.henerypress.com

Trade Paperback ISBN-13: 978-1-63511-187-3
Digital epub ISBN-13: 978-1-63511-188-0
Kindle ISBN-13: 978-1-63511-189-7
Hardcover Paperback ISBN-13: 978-1-63511-190-3

Printed in the United States of America

For my cousin Mike Godbey.
Thank you for always being there for Daddy.

ACKNOWLEDGMENTS

I'm blessed to have amazing readers who embrace the Southern mysteries I love to write.

Thank you Dianne Jessie for helping me name *Fixin' To Die*, the first book in the Kenni Lowry Mystery Series. It's perfect! Cyndy Ranzau, you are amazing and so awesome to bounce ideas off of.

Chapter One

"Someone cooked his goose and cooked it good." Poppa squatted next to the lifeless body Myrna Savage had found in her greenhouse, right on top of her tomato plants. The body had on jeans and a dark blue hoodie with the hood still pulled up over the head, the face smashed right down into a pile of tomatoes—so we couldn't tell whether it was a man or a woman. "Peee-uuu." Poppa pinched his nose with one hand and waved the space in front of his face with the other. "Where are his shoes?"

It took everything I had not to shush him, since everyone was staring at me for guidance and since they couldn't see the ghost of Elmer Sims. Not only was Elmer the ex-sheriff of my small town of Cottonwood, Kentucky, but also my grandfather, who'd come back in ghost form to be my guardian when I became sheriff. I was the only one who could see—or hear—him.

"Why did he have to fall on my prize tomatoes?" Myrna Savage lifted her hands up to the sides of her head and tugged a little at the edges of her dark hair.

She moved without haste over to the greenhouse window, where the juice and seeds from the squished tomatoes had splattered and dripped down the glass. She pointed her finger at the very dead facedown body. Flattened tomatoes stuck halfway out from underneath the body. Myrna's lips contorted to the left and to the right before she brought her fists up to the side of her body and thrust them back down.

"It took me months to get them that plump," she protested.

"Myrna, I know you're upset." I put my hand out to stop her from moving all over the place and tainting the scene.

"Upset?" she wailed. "That's an understatement. Do you know how long it takes to grow prize tomatoes such as those squished up under that body?"

"Until we can determine what happened, that body is going to stay right there." I clenched my jaw and lifted my eyes to meet her icy stare. I gripped the handle of my police bag that I always kept ready in my Wagoneer.

"I can tell you what happened to that body." Myrna pointed. "They came into my greenhouse and keeled over right on my prize tomatoes."

"We don't know anything for sure." I bent down and used my finger to slightly move the hood so I could try to feel for a pulse on the neck.

"Turn 'em over. See who it is." Poppa stood next to Myrna. I ignored him. There was a protocol, and I was going to follow it as sheriff. Just in case the person was alive, we didn't move a body in fear it would harm them more.

No pulse.

I stood up and looked at Finn.

"Who are you?" Myrna asked in a grudging voice. Her eyes slid past my shoulder and fixed on Finn Vincent, my new deputy.

"I'm Officer Finn Vincent from the State Reserve." Finn took his wallet out of his back pocket and flipped the badge at her. "I've been helping Sheriff Lowry over the past few days since Lonnie Lemar retired."

"Lonnie retired months ago," she snarled. "You mean you helped Kenni solve the murder of Doc Walton?"

No one could put anything past Myrna Savage. Her name was fitting. She was a long-time widow who owned Petal Pushers Landscaping. She hired many people I wouldn't trust to take care of Duke, my dog. But Myrna wasn't scared of anyone, and if they crossed her, they better watch out. I couldn't help but wonder if this person had crossed her in some way.

The faint sound of an ambulance echoed in the dark.

"Gosh darn," Myra snapped. "'Bout time they got here. I called them first and you second."

Finn hadn't been formerly deputized since the mayor had offered him the open deputy's job we had in the sheriff's department. Luckily, in the state of Kentucky, I could use my power to deputize on the spot. Now was as good a time as any.

"By Kentucky law PC 150, I hereby deputize you, Finley Vincent, to the Cottonwood Sheriff's Department." My words were swift. The mayor had already told Finn the job was his and was going to officially swear him in later in the week. I was just helping it along. "Myrna Savage is a witness to this appointment until we can go before the judge."

I looked at Myrna.

"What?" she snarled.

"Say okay." I helped her along.

"Okay," she responded.

The ambulance light flooded the lawn and made a spotlight on the greenhouse. Two EMTs rushed over with their medical bags and immediately felt for a pulse. Both of them looked at each other before they slid their eyes up to me.

They confirmed what I already knew.

The death stare. Something I'd gotten used to seeing over the past few weeks. Slowly they shook their heads. They stepped outside of the greenhouse and started filling out some paperwork.

Finn and I looked at each other for a second before we bent

down over the body, both of us knowing what was coming next. I took the shoulder region and Finn the legs.

"On three." I sucked in a deep breath of dread before I began to count.

After we flipped the body, both of us stood up, looking down.

"Well, I'll be." Poppa stood at the man's head. "It's Owen Godbey. What on earth did he do to anyone?"

"Do you know him?" Finn asked.

"Owen Godbey. He's Myrna's delivery man." I acted as if I knew the man. I had seen Owen a handful of times around town delivering flowers for Myrna, but he and the rest of the Godbey crew kept to themselves out on Catnip Road. Never in any trouble that I could recall. "Maybe he had a heart attack or something," I said as I took my first good look at his body.

There were no visible signs of blood anywhere and no signs of trauma. Simply a man that was clothed without shoes, with tomato seeds on his face and imbedded in his mustache. He'd been there for some time.

Myrna's hand flew up to her mouth as her eyes descended on Owen. She gasped. "Is he really d...d..."

"I'm sorry, Myrna." I took off my hat to give my condolences and showed her the door of the greenhouse. "I know Owen was your only employee and I'm sorry."

Finn followed us out.

"But he's not supposed to be in there." She shook her head. "I mean, it's late."

"Finn, can you give Max Bogus a call and let him know that we have a body?" I stuck my hat back on my head. "Myrna, you stay here."

I walked back into the greenhouse and took a closer look at Owen and considered what my poppa's ghost was insisting. My gut told me this was no accident.

Chapter Two

"Myrna." I took a deep breath and set my police bag on the dirt floor, bending down to get out a pair of gloves after she'd walked back in with Finn. "Can you tell me what you were doing when you discovered the body?"

"I was working on my tomato salad recipe," she said matter-of-factly. "I am going to enter it into the cook-off. But Kenni, there is a body right there." She wrung her hands and told me something I already could see.

"Myrna, I know this is upsetting, but it's crucial you give me all the details leading up to when you discovered the body." I put a reassuring hand on her arm. "Now, what cook-off?" I asked, wondering if a salad would even qualify.

I hadn't heard of a cook-off being held. There weren't too many kept secrets around here. Especially anything that involved food.

"Between Jolee and Ben." She straightened her shoulders. Pride glowed in her green eyes. "I'm team Jolee."

My brows furrowed.

"While you've been off solving crimes, Jolee and Ben's competitive streaks have been going ninety miles an hour." Myrna talked ninety miles an hour. "They're hosting a friendly food competition. They had people apply and cook something for them. They each picked a team of three. This week they'll pick the winner of their three. The finalists on each team will go up against each other. Whoever wins gets a monthly licensing fee along with their dish served at both restaurants. I'm making my family's secret tomato salad recipe with my prize tomatoes that Owen just took out."

"But I thought you were in the flower contest up in Lexington this week." That I did hear.

Myrna raised the most beautiful flowers in her greenhouse. She was the only florist in Cottonwood, so we didn't have much choice when it came to buying flowers. She even owned the floral department space at Dixon's Foodtown, our local grocery store. Story went she and Mr. Dixon had a bet late one night. I hadn't heard what they were betting on, but I did hear that he lost and Myrna won a contract to be the only florist in his store.

"Kenni Lowry, have you been checking up on poor old Myrna?" she asked.

"Obviously not good enough," I mumbled, because I hadn't heard of any cook-off and I was a frequent diner at both places.

She scurried next to the counter and practically threw herself down next to the body. She stuck her hand up underneath the counter and pulled out a tomato just as plump as a peach. "You didn't get this one!" She shook the tomato at the body before she bounced up and brushed herself off.

Myrna's odd behavior and her concern of her tomatoes over the body didn't sit well.

"Well, Myrna, if listening to idle gossip in the front pew of the Cottonwood Baptist Church on a Sunday morning waiting for Preacher to give me a weekly dose of Jesus is checking up on you, then I guess you can say that I'm checking up on you and all the fine citizens of our community." I snapped the gloves on my hands and held a pair to hand to Finn. "Now if you could answer my question."

"Um-hmm. What question was that?"

Myrna rubbed the tomato like a newborn baby's butt.

"Let's step outside." I had to get her out of the greenhouse before she contaminated any more evidence at the scene.

"The flower show?" I asked again as I led her out.

Poppa followed my every move. He cocked his head to the side, listening intently to Myrna as though he were hanging on her every word.

"Oh, yes. Of course I'm doing the flower show." She shot a penetrating look my way.

"Both?" I found it odd that Myrna suddenly had a lot of time on her hands.

"The flower show is one weekend, whereas the cook-off spans a week," Myrna said.

"What about the van?" I gestured toward the delivery van outside the greenhouse that Myrna had wrapped with images of flower arrangements. "Would Owen have been delivering flowers and come in here?"

"I told you, it's late and he didn't have any deliveries." She chewed on her bottom lip. She tilted her head to the side and looked back into the greenhouse.

"Besides, he liked to use his truck on most delivery days. He said something about not having to get a ride back to his house."

Finn walked out of the greenhouse. "I hate to interrupt this questioning, but, Ms. Savage, there is smoke coming out of your house window." He gestured toward Myrna's house, where black smoke was billowing out of an open window.

"My stewed tomatoes!" She shoved past Finn, nearly knocking him down as she ran through her backyard with the plump tomato held gingerly in the palm of her hand.

Finn and I took the opportunity to comb the crime scene without Myrna keeping watch.

Poppa had already gone back inside of the greenhouse and assessed the scene in his own ghostly way.

It was dark. When I had gotten the call about Myrna finding the body, Finn and I were sitting on the Ferris wheel at the annual Cottonwood festival at the fairgrounds. I was looking into his big brown eyes as he told me the picture of the beautiful brunette in his wallet was not his girlfriend, but his sister, which sent my heart into a tailspin. Something I wasn't really expecting. And if I wasn't mistaken, on the downswing of the Ferris wheel, Finn Vincent was about to ask me out on a real date. Then we got interrupted by the call.

Owen's murder, if it was one, would be the third crime that'd happened in Cottonwood over the last few weeks. To some small towns or even big cities, that might seem to be a little low on the crime side, but not in Cottonwood.

"This is so odd," Finn noted. "There isn't a lot here to go on."

I looked around and retraced our steps, taking a few notes. With Myrna out of the greenhouse, I took the time to talk to Finn. "There isn't a weapon. There isn't much blood splatter. And there is no sign of a struggle." This was very unusual for a crime scene. "Which makes me believe that he was dumped here," I said and continued to make notes on the notepad.

"Someone wants us to believe that Myrna did it." Finn rocked back on his heels. "But that her attitude went from being upset to suddenly only caring about her tomatoes is also worth noting, and disturbing."

"I noticed that too." I looked out the door when I heard Myrna's feet stomping back down to the greenhouse.

I walked out of the greenhouse with my bag in my hand and let Finn have a few more minutes alone in there without Myrna eyeballing our every move.

"Do you have any idea why he might be here?" I asked Myrna when she came back from tending to her stewed tomatoes.

"Well, we were both on Jolee's team and we each have to come up with our own recipe." She bit the edge of her lip and looked around my shoulder into the greenhouse, not once taking her eyes off of Finn. "Do you think he was trying to sabotage me? Steal my 'mators, and then he had a heart attack?"

Finn walked out and took my bag from me.

"You never know. Anything is possible," I said. Finn took the camera out of my bag and walked back in the greenhouse to take some photos. We were going to treat this like a crime scene until we figured out how Owen died.

"He was so jealous of my tomatoes and how good they were growing. I could see it on his face when we met with Jolee." Myrna picked at the edges of her nails. "I thought his recipe was stupid. Okra."

My mouth watered. I did love a good southern fried okra.

"Rae Lynn did make a mighty fine okra dish." Poppa licked his chops and rubbed his hands together as he recalled Owen's mama's recipe.

"Jolee questioned him about it too since she already makes that okra burger everyone loves." Myrna nervously talked and talked. Her voice rose an octave. "Now Viola is the only thing standing between me and the prize."

"Viola White?" I asked, looking her over with a critical eye. I had a niggling suspicion she was keeping something from me.

"Yes. Me, Owen, and Viola are Team Jolee." Her face was stone-cold serious. "Now with Owen out of the way, I'm sure I can beat Viola."

I couldn't help but think that if it did turn out Owen Godbey had been murdered, Myrna had just handed me a motive.

Chapter Three

"Evening, Sheriff." Max Bogus walked by me and Myrna with his briefcase and his usual attire of khaki pants and a blue button-down shirt. "Myrna."

"It's not a good evening, Max Bogus," Myrna quipped. "Any time you find a dead body in your greenhouse is not a good time."

"Excuse me for a minute, Myrna." I excused myself to follow Max into the greenhouse to give him the update, stopping when I felt Myrna hot on my heels. "You stay out here," I instructed her, which made her none too happy.

She opened her mouth to protest. I gave her the wonky eye. She closed her mouth and sucked in a deep breath.

Max and I walked in. "Owen Godbey," he noted, sticking the case on the counter next to a few glass vases.

He opened his case and took out a clipboard and a pair of gloves before he bent down to take a look at the body. He made notes and took measurements and his own photos before retrieving the church cart. Finn held the door as Max wheeled Owen's body out of the greenhouse.

We stopped shy of Max's hearse. Poppa stood next to us, taking it all in. It was critical for Max to determine if Owen's death was due to natural causes or a homicide.

"Well..." Max rubbed the top of his head, his eyes encased behind thick spectacles. "I found some little burn holes around his ankles. I'm not sure what those are. I have an idea, but I'm not real sure. So for now, I can't say this is natural causes."

"Give me a call when you have the autopsy scheduled." I looked from Max to Finn. It was law that any time a body was found under unnatural circumstances, there had to be an autopsy. I gave Finn the slow nod that he knew meant we had to secure the scene.

"I'll get started on him first thing in the morning. I should have some preliminary results in the afternoon, but I'll call Betty and let her know." He referred to Betty Murphy, my dispatch operator. "Unless you want to be there when I perform it?"

"No, no." The sooner I got this one solved, the better. After all, re-election was only a couple of years away, and I didn't want to lose my job or my Poppa's ghost. Poppa and I knew he was here in a ghost-deputy capacity to not only try to help me from the great beyond, but also to keep me safe. Both of us figured he was here because of the crime and we were afraid if I wasn't sheriff, he wouldn't be here. "I've got some leads I need to follow up on." I had to go see Jolee and talk to her about Owen and Myrna's interaction in the competition.

"I know it's late and this has been a long night for everyone." I tried to smile. "Myrna, you can go on in for the night. Finn and I are going to secure the scene while Max takes Owen on down to the morgue."

"But what about my tomatoes? I need to get my salad made up before I go into town tomorrow to see Jolee." She blinked at me in bafflement.

"You are going to have to use Dixon's tomatoes for your recipe," I stated.

"Well, I never." She put her hand to her chest and drew in a big breath. On the exhale, she bellowed, "You think that's okay? It's clearly not. This is a competition and I have to have my prize tomatoes. What would your mama say about your manners?"

"Not tonight or anytime soon are you going back into that greenhouse." Times like these I found it hard to be the sheriff of the town I grew up in. Before I even did something, my mama already knew about it. In this case, I was one-hundred percent sure the first thing Myrna Savage was going to do was go in her house and dial my mama directly.

Myrna gave a few huffs and puffs before she turned on the balls of her feet and stormed right back up to her house.

By the time I turned back around, Max had Owen's body covered on the church cart. Finn had used evidence markers to mark off some spots, along with dusting for fingerprints.

"It's going to be a long night, Kenni-bug." My Poppa's face was all lit up. He always loved being sheriff, especially when there was a crime to be solved.

"We don't even know if he was murdered," I whispered, under my breath so Max or Finn wouldn't hear me.

"Oh, it was murder alright." Poppa's voice was tight as he spoke. "Them burn holes around his ankles." The grin on his face sent chills all over my body. "High-grade barbwire electric fence."

"No one uses that kind of fencing anymore." I knew Poppa was a great sheriff, but I hadn't seen anyone use barbwire electric fence around here since I was a kid.

"Someone does." Poppa's gaze came to rest on my questioning face. You'd think this would've been a time that him being a ghost would come in handy. But he was really here as my guardian, to keep me safe in my job and help me solve crimes. He wasn't all-knowing. His voice cut the silence. "Those burn holes are spaced twelve inches apart. If you look at the holes around his ankles and wrap a couple feet of barbwire around him, they will match right on up."

"Well, we're out of here." Max rolled Owen past me.

"Wait a second." I walked over to the church cart. While

Max opened the hatch of the hearse, I pulled the blanket off of Owen's feet. As gross as it might sound, I bent down and took a whiff. Owen Godbey's feet were as clean as a peeled egg. Not a speck of dirt, piece of grass, or even a bit of stink.

"What are you looking for?" Max asked me.

"I was looking to see if he walked here." I pointed to the clean piggies. "He must have been placed here or thrown in the greenhouse." I pointed to Owen's ankles. "The burn marks. Do they look like barbwire electric fence burns?" I asked.

Max's jaw dropped. He didn't have to say another word.

"Max, it looks like we have another homicide." The sound of my own voice was a blow to my chest. My gut sank remembering the last homicide.

My eyes clung to Max's as I analyzed his reaction.

"You might be on to something." He simply shook his head. He walked to the front of the hearse but turned back around. He pointed directly at me. "It takes a mean son of a you-know-what to kill a man using electric fencing, if that is the case."

I felt Max's anger as much as I saw it.

I stood there and watched Max drive off with Owen in the back before I walked back into the greenhouse.

"Anything?" I asked Finn about the fingerprints he was lifting on the back door of the greenhouse.

"There are a couple sets of prints. I'm guessing that both are accounted for. One being Myrna's and the other Owen's." He had put a sticky marker on the door and the handle. "The handle and the door look to be same prints just by my naked eye, but we'll run them anyways."

"Do you have a gut feeling?" In this business, when something like this happened, there was generally one. I looked around, careful where I stepped.

He shook his head. "I'm not familiar with the citizens here and I'm going to have to listen to your direction." He smiled that fancy white smile and made my heart go pitter-patter. "You okay?"

"Thinking." I looked around the crime scene. "Owen worked for her, but they are in this competition. She came outside and saw the body." I paced back and forth. "One problem: if she did it, how did she kill him? Those burn holes around his ankles are likely from an electric fence that keeps anything or anyone out of the herd. It's not just a little bitty shock, though you really don't need a big shock to go into cardiac arrest." I looked around and then through the back door, where Poppa was doing a little investigating on his own. I had learned that murder investigations were like a puzzle. There were pieces here, but how did they all fit together? "If he was killed by the electric fence, then how on earth did Myrna Savage wrangle him to the ground to do it?"

Like I said, Myrna was a savage, but not in the physical way. She was a grudge holder. It only took a person one time to wrong Myrna for her to hold it against you and your kin for the rest of her life and theirs. She was a short stack that couldn't wrangle a garden snake, much less a man the size of Owen Godbey.

"How big would you say Owen Godbey is? Was?" I asked Finn.

"I'd say he was a good two-fifty." Finn confirmed my thoughts. "There's no way she took him down."

"Plus, I don't recall Myrna ever having livestock. There would be no reason to have an electric fence." I had a quick thought. "Tomorrow I'll head on down to the Tractor Supply and see if anyone has bought any electric fencing lately."

Cottonwood was too small for someone not to notice. My guess was that not many people were buying barbwire these days, much less electric fencing, since electric netting had become so popular.

"This is definitely a crime of passion if someone would go as far as truly making sure he was dead by using electric fencing." The thought of it boggled my mind. I really shouldn't have been surprised because as a sheriff, I'd seen a lot, just not in Cottonwood. "They would've had to get the wire around his ankle before they turned on the electric charge. So was he passed out first or killed first?"

"Good question." Finn looked down at the body. His eyes slide up to mine. "How did you even think of barbwire fencing?" Finn asked.

"It was divine intervention," I teased, glancing over his shoulder to where Poppa was still outside looking around. "Did you notice anything outside?"

"I haven't gotten that far." Finn continued to poke around the greenhouse.

It was my chance to get to snoop. I went outside with Poppa.

"Can't see a whole lot out here in the dark." Poppa used the sole of his shoe to brush across the tall grass.

"I think we're going to have to wait until daylight, but I can go to Owen's house to see if anything is out of sorts." I glanced around the grass on my way back to tell Finn he could go on back to his hotel room. The city had been renting it for him since he'd been here helping out with Doc's murder.

Something crunched underneath my shoe. I stopped. My flashlight was in my bag inside, and since I'd been in street clothes at the festival, I didn't have on my utility belt. I took my cell out of my back pocket and turned on the flashlight feature, shining it toward the ground.

As soon as my light hit the ground, a small triangle shimmered. It was some sort of colored glass.

"What's that?" Finn questioned from the back door.

"I'm not sure." I pointed to a pair of gloves Finn had folded over out of his jeans pocket. He handed them to me and I slipped them on before I bent down and picked up the glass. I palmed it and walked inside the greenhouse.

Finn held open an evidence baggie for me. "It might be something."

I opened my fingers and let the glass fall into the baggie. It was like slow motion as my brain tried to figure out where I'd seen something like this before.

"Are you okay?" Finn asked. "It must be hard being from a small town and seeing someone you know murdered."

"It's not that." My eyes drew up to meet his steely gaze. "I have seen something like this before, but I can't place it."

"Think." Poppa stood next to me, encouraging me. "Use that noggin."

"Like I said before, all the clues are here. We just have to wait for them to talk to us." Finn logged in the evidence. "I guess we can wait until morning. I've got everything I think we need bagged up and ready to be sent off. I'll be sure to have it sent to the lab." His cell chirped from his pocket and he answered, telling the other person he'd be right over. "That was Lulu McClain. She said she heard I was going to be staying a while and offered me the apartment above the boutique."

"I bet hotel living is getting old." I smiled, knowing Lulu McClain was a dirty old woman who wanted to make Finn her lemon bars and watch him go goo-goo over them.

He checked his watch. "If I hurry, I can grab my stuff and move in tonight."

That was my cue to get him back to the fairgrounds where we'd left his car. Finn was right about the clues being under our nose. But what were they? Who would want Owen Godbey dead and why? Owen knew something, but what?

Chapter Four

It was strange to talk to my Poppa's ghost. Sometimes it was surreal. I gripped the steering wheel of my old Wagoneer, which had been his. He sat in the passenger side and hung on to the door as we rattled our way down Catnip, where the Godbeys had their compound. Owen and his brother, Stanley, lived on adjoining properties. It was rumored that Stanley got Rae Lynn's house when she died. I wasn't sure what Owen had gotten, but it was worth looking into in case there was a family rift.

In the dead of the night, I could talk to anyone I pleased and no one would see me. But in the daylight I had to be more cautious. It wouldn't take but one person seeing me carrying on a conversation with myself to start a rumor that the sheriff had gone and fell off the cuckoo wagon. Especially during election season.

The sheriff position was an elected four-year term in the great state of Kentucky. I was honored and grateful to be able to serve the people who made me who I was today. But if an elected official made those people mad, they didn't care what your roots were. They'd turn on you in a minute; you'd be gone. Outcast. And in my case, I was the first female sheriff ever elected in Cottonwood, which made things a little more difficult when it came to solving things like murder. Some old timers still didn't think it was fittin' for a girl to be sticking her nose in a crime scene.

They didn't mind a gun-totin' one. That was common around these parts—if you didn't have a gun, then something was wrong with you. But a girl playing cop was another story. That wasn't common.

"You might want to give Stanley a holler." Poppa was good at reminding me of things I needed to do and the order I needed to do them in.

"I know, Poppa. I've been doing this for some time now." I took a right onto Catnip Road, one of our most dangerous roads with all its hairpin curves, even though it wasn't considered to be in the country part of our town.

Owen lived pretty far off the road, down a gravel driveway.

"You might know to go to the next of kin, but I bet you don't know the Godbeys own almost two thousand acres of these woods." He peered out the window of the old Wagoneer. The woods were on both sides of the road.

"Do they farm?" I asked. "Or hunt?"

Those were the two main reasons people owned land in Cottonwood.

"They did a lot of okra planting as far back as I could remember." Poppa's voice was deep and dusty. "Though I can't recall if the boys continued to grow the crop after Rae Lynn died, about four years before me."

I glanced over. It was just plain eerie hearing Poppa talk about his death. And a time I didn't want to remember.

We pulled in to the driveway. I could see Owen's trailer was one of those that could just hitch up to a truck and haul out at any given notice.

"All this land and that tiny trailer." I shook my head and put the Wagoneer in park.

"Do you know where Sandy moved?" Poppa asked about Owen's ex-wife.

"No. I need to interview her." A line formed between my brows.

Recently at my girl's Euchre night, I'd heard some rumblings that Sandy and Owen still hadn't finalized their divorce. Of course, it was during the gossip session between taking trump at the Euchre table, but still, it was noteworthy now.

Owen was older than me. Even though Cottonwood was small, our paths rarely crossed, unless there was a festival or he happened to come to a town-council meeting. I'd certainly forgotten about the wedding and their divorce until now. I remembered I'd also heard at the Euchre table that Sandy had moved as soon as they signed the separation papers.

I got out of the Jeep and reached over to grab my bag. Poppa ghosted himself out of the truck and over to the driver's side. I grabbed my bag off the floorboard and slipped my phone in my back pocket before I shut the car door.

I put the bag on top of the hood and stuck my fists on my hips. "I wonder how on Earth Owen got to the greenhouse. Or more importantly, who took him to the greenhouse." I hesitated, bewildered. "It would make sense if he was using the Petal Pusher van for deliveries because he'd been driving it. But according to Myrna, he wasn't working and he liked to use his truck for deliveries."

"We're going to figure this out," Poppa assured me. "We always do."

Poppa's death had been really hard for me. We were so close, and the times I came home from college, it was to see him. Not that I didn't love visiting my parents. But every time, my mom seized the opportunity to try and talk me out of being a police officer. She wanted me to leave the academy to come home to Cottonwood, where she'd love to see me be in the Sweet Adelines, a Baptist Women's church group, a teller at a local bank, a wife, and a mother—which all sounded a lot like her.

Instead, she'd had to settle for me being elected sheriff, joining the Euchre club, and every now and then throwing back a couple of beers.

"I'm glad I'm here to help out still." Poppa smiled back at me.

"Since you're here as my guardian while I'm wearing this badge, we have to solve this crime fast." My heart tugged. It had been so hard having him gone. Since I'd gotten him back, I didn't want to imagine life without him. "Because I'm not ready to lose my job or you."

"Then let's get to it." He vigorously rubbed his hands together.

"Tell me about Sandy," I encouraged him as I took the flashlight out of my bag and shined it all around the darkness. Unfortunately, it was almost too dark for me to see anything.

"From what I heard, pure speculation from some of the Sweet Adelines who use to bring me suppers," he leaned in and winked, "Sandy had been a Sweet Adeline and when she left Owen, the girls said something about there being jealousy between Sandy and her sister-in-law." Poppa snapped his fingers. "Umm...umm..."

"Inez?" I questioned.

He jutted his pointer finger toward me. "That's it." He tapped his temple. "The old memory is still going a little."

"I couldn't imagine Inez being jealous of anyone." It was out of character from what I remembered of her. She was the bank teller that my mama so desperately wanted me to be. She always greeted me with a smile when I came in. "I guess I need to find out where Sandy is and check into this."

Not that I was sure either of them had anything to do with

Owen's death, since it still wasn't an official homicide. But they might have leads on who hung out with Owen, or even who might have a grudge against him so bad that they wanted him dead, in case it was a murder as I suspected. By the looks of Owen's ankles, I was pretty positive he didn't do that to himself. Inez and Stanley had both retired. She should be easy to track down.

"Why the hell not, Kenni-bug?" Poppa smacked his thigh. "Right now you should think everyone that had even an inkling of a conversation with Owen is a suspect."

My phone chirped from my pocket. I pulled it out and saw a text from Finn.

"Those darn cell phones," Poppa spat. "Who in the world can't wait for you to get home?"

"It's Finn." I tried to hide the smile from seeing his name scroll across my phone. "He just moved into the apartment above Lulu's Boutique and Lulu already made him a big Kentucky Derby Pie."

"Are you smiling because of the thought of how delicious that pie is or because it's a message from him?" Poppa questioned. "I'd understand if you were smiling about Lulu's pie because it is to die for. But that boy..." Poppa hesitated. "I've seen those boys before. I'm not saying I don't like him. I do, Kenni-bug, but as a partner, not a lover."

"Poppa!" My mouth flew open. My face felt hot from embarrassment.

"I know it's nothing you want to discuss with your Poppa, much less your dead one, but these cops from big cities come in and think they want to get involved in the small community, which they do with good intentions." Poppa sucked in a deep breath. "But when there is little to no crime or excitement, they start to get restless and itch to go back home to the hustle and bustle of the fast pace crime-ridden world they are used to."

"Well, you don't have to worry about that," I lied, annoyed that Poppa planted that seed in my head. "You know me. Mama and Daddy's good, well-mannered southern girl who will extend hospitality to anyone."

I also wanted to say that Mama was the one who had begun to plant romantic ideas about Finn in my head. As much as I had tried to push back on Mama's idea of me and Finn, the idea pushed back on me.

"As long as that's all it is." Poppa looked at me out of the corner of his eye, but I continued to squat down and look under Owen's truck with the flashlight.

The thought of Sandy and Inez made my gut twirl. They would know who Owen talked to or even who he complained about.

"Let's go on in." I headed toward the trailer and walked up the two cement blocks he used as steps. I knocked on the door with the butt of the flashlight. "Sheriff. Open up."

Poppa and I waited to see if anyone came to the door. I leaned my ear in and listened for footsteps.

I tapped again and said a little louder, "Last time. This is Sheriff Lowry and I'm coming in."

I glanced back at Poppa and he nodded. Him giving me the go-ahead felt so much better than me doing it on my own. I put my hand on the doorknob and tried to turn it. It was locked.

I took my keys, where I had kept a bump key for times just like now.

"This is a bump key—a basic key that can open most door locks. The academy teaches you that you should keep one on your belt in case you need to get into a door and quickly. And since Owen is a victim in our case, we can enter without a warrant."

"Things sure are different than since I had my police training." Poppa scratched his head.

Within seconds, I was standing inside the small trailer and found the light switch, illuminating the inside. There was an old leather couch that looked all dried up with cracks popping along the seams. There was a beat-up coffee table with an old *Guns and Gear* magazine with torn edges and a coffee cup halfway filled with coffee on top. To the far right was a card table set up with a two-burner hot plate on it, along with the coffee pot. I put my hand on the pot. It was cold to the touch. I knew Owen liked coffee as much as me, because when I did see him, he always had a cup in his hand. But not tonight. Next to the pot were a few empty bottles of medication prescribed by Doctor Camille Shively.

I headed back toward the end of the small trailer. There was a single mattress lying on the floor and an old quilt knotted up on top of it.

"He lived pretty simple. No wonder he worked delivering flowers. I couldn't imagine he was making much." I shrugged.

"Both boys got what they wanted, from what I'd heard." Poppa referred to Owen's mama.

"What did they want?" I asked.

"That I don't know, but I do know that Rae Lynn and Ruby Smith were close." That was a good bit of information. Ruby Smith would be more than willing to do a little gossiping.

I took out my phone and typed her name in my notes. I was in need of a new clock, and since I had gotten my last one at Ruby's Antiques, it was only fittin' to get my next one there.

"Nothing looks out of place, which makes me think that the end of Owen's life didn't happen here." I looked around the small trailer again. "I'll put up some crime tape and secure the trailer and his truck in case there's something here we can't see in the dark."

"Sounds good," Poppa said before he disappeared. It was a trick he was good at. One minute he was there and the next he wasn't. I locked the door behind me and trotted down the cement blocks before the feeling of someone watching me knotted around me. I clicked my flashlight on and shined it all around, anticipating I was going to see glowing eyes from afar. When I saw nothing, I chalked it up to a very active imagination due to the fact I had a feeling there was a killer was among us. Within minutes I had taken the crime tape from my bag and stuck it all over the trailer door and around Owen's truck. I made sure the tape was along the creases of the doors so if someone did try to get in the trailer or truck, they'd have to break the tape.

Before I could go home and let Duke out, I knew I had to go see Stanley Godbey. He was Owen's next of kin in Cottonwood that I knew of, since I didn't know where Sandy was.

Stanley and Inez's house was a few acres over from Owen's. They too had a gravel drive that went way back on the property. Most people who lived off of Catnip Road had gravel. It was just too expensive to get a blacktop driveway, and concrete wasn't an option because it cracked so much easier and had to be replaced. So the luxury of a blacktop drive made sense only if you could afford it. By the looks of things, Stanley could afford it.

His house was much different than Owen's hook-up trailer. It was an actual two-story home with a wraparound porch covered by a tin roof. The bottom half of the house was covered in stone, real stone, not the fake stuff, and there were three dormer windows on the top floor. Next to the house was a steel barn, the kind you could take down and move around if you had to. But by the looks of the tall grass around the base of the barn, Stanley hadn't used his Weed Eater in a while.

The front porch light flipped on, and it wasn't on an automatic timer, because the front wooden door flung open too. It wasn't just a wooden front door; it was a custom door with the most beautiful glass cross inlaid in the middle. I could see where

Owen could be a little envious of Stanley if this was the house he'd inherited.

"Sheriff." Stanley stood about six feet tall. He was bald, by choice from what I'd heard down at Tiny Tina's, because he was too cheap to pay for a haircut. But by the looks of their property, there was no way he couldn't afford a fifteen-dollar trim. "It's awfully late for you to be making a friendly call, so that means there's somethin' wrong." His steel-blue eyes zeroed in on me. "Is this official? You don't have on your uniform."

"I'm sorry to come by so late. I was at the festival when I got a call that Myrna Savage found a body in her greenhouse."

I walked up onto the porch. Over his shoulder I could see Inez turn a corner and walk down the hall that led to the door. Her brown hair was parted down the middle and pulled back in a low ponytail, exactly how she'd worn it every time I'd seen her at the bank. The usual skirt suit I'd seen her in was replaced by a pair of jeans and a conservative pullover white sweater. Small diamond stud earrings twinkled from her earlobes. Her bare feet showed her toenails were painted a pretty pearl.

"Kenni?" she questioned when our eyes met. "Oh no. What's wrong, Stan?"

"I'm sorry to tell you that your brother, Owen, was found dead in Myrna's greenhouse. At this time, we are investigating his death and I'm not going to lie. It looks suspicious." This was the part of the job that never got easy. No matter how I delivered the news about a death—although it was usually of natural causes—it was the immediate reaction on the loved ones' faces that made me pause.

Immediately, and unexpectedly, Inez let out an audible groan, her hands flew to her open mouth, and she curled over at the waist. Stanley put a hand on her back to try to comfort her.

"I'm not surprised if someone did kill him," were Stanley Godbey's first words after hearing of Owen's death.

"Excuse me?" I questioned, a little taken aback.

"The way he lived." Stanley shook his head. "He didn't take care of himself. He was always asking for money for his medication."

"That's still no reason for someone to kill him," Inez bit back. "Oh, Kenni, how?"

"We aren't sure he was killed. I'm just saying it looks suspicious so we are doing an autopsy to rule anything out. Max has his body at the morgue, so I'm going to have to ask you to go down and identify him." That was the second thing I hated to tell people about their loved one. "Do you know what medications he was on?"

Inez cleared her throat. Both of them shook their heads.

"God." Stanley ran his hand over his shiny bald head. "I knew he was going to get in trouble."

Inez shushed him.

"Do you know if anyone had a grudge against him?" I asked, hoping they'd offer up some information I didn't have to dig for. "You know I'm just covering all my bases."

"Sandy." Inez's lashes drew down, making a shadow on her cheeks.

"Enough." Stanley put his hand out to shut Inez up.

"She wanted that cookbook. She wanted him dead." Inez nodded her head and then pinched her lips when she saw the look on Stanley's face.

"What cookbook?" I questioned, hoping for some more clues.

"Nothing." Stanley's voice sharpened.

"Stanley, if you know something, in case this is a homicide, I need to know." I rocked back on the heels of my cowboy boots and planted my hands to my side. I was going to have to play hard ball with Stanley Godbey, who I'd heard wasn't a person to mess with.

"We don't know nothin'," he said with easy defiance. "Inez here is talking out of school. We don't air out our dirty laundry to no one, especially the police. And he never exercised. I kept telling him that since he was single he needed to take better care of himself. It could have been a heart attack."

"Stan." Inez put her hand on his forearm. He jerked it away. She pulled back, took a deep breath, and curled her shoulders backward. "Thank you for stopping by, Kenni. We'll go in the morning to identify Owen's remains. As you can see, this is a shock to us and we need to process what's happened."

I wasn't sure, but I think she just blessed my heart without saying it.

"I'm going to let you have peace tonight, but I do expect you to come down to the office and answer some questions tomorrow." My brows lifted and I boldly met Stan's gaze.

"You tell your mama and them we said hello." The door shut in my face. Behind the cross, I could see the Godbeys nose to nose and I couldn't help but wonder what all the secrets were about. When Inez brought up Sandy and the cookbook, things got icy.

Chapter Five

My phone chirped a text when I made it back to the Jeep. Finn wanted to know if I'd found anything out at the trailer, then asked if I wanted to stop by and have a piece of Derby pie before he ate it all.

Poppa's voice echoed into my head about how cops like Finn got restless in small towns, the itch they got to go back to where they'd come from.

I chewed on Finn's offer as the Wagoneer rambled down the gravel driveway and back into town. Lulu's Boutique was on the north end of town and it just so happened I had to go through the north side to get to Free Row where I lived.

A shiver of recollection of me and Finn sitting in the buggy of the Ferris wheel a few short hours ago breezed through my mind. If Poppa was right and if Finn did have an itch, I was going to try and scratch it while he was here.

Before I could even protest my own thoughts and replace them with the reasonable cop side of my brain, the Wagoneer had pulled up to the curb right outside of the small clapboard house Lulu McClain had turned into a cute shop selling locally made knick-knacks, candles, crocks, rag rugs, fashionable scarves, chunky jewels, bath salts, and much more.

She had a craft room, or what Lulu herself called a craft room—I liked to refer to it as the gossip suite. Lulu hosted all sorts of girlfriend events like canvas painting, wine tasting, ceramics, and Mary Kay parties, as well as Shabby Trends. This week our Euchre group was meeting here.

Quickly I looked in the rearview and ran my hand down my honey-colored hair and pinched some color back into my tired cheeks. There was no hope for the bags that'd settled under my green eyes.

"Back here," I heard Finn call when I got out of the Jeep.

He stood near the entrance to the craft room. He had on a white t-shirt and pair of jeans. He was barefooted, like Owen Godbey, and held a beer in his hand.

"Did you find anything?" He held the beer out. "Come on in and get a beer. I had enough time to not only grab my little bag of clothes from the motel but also a six pack."

I followed him up the back steps to the apartment, trying not to focus on his broad shoulders and muscles that were clearly taunting me through that white tee. The edges of his dark hair were brushing the collar of the tee, a little too long for how I was sure Finn liked his hair. I stood in the threshold of the apartment, trying to talk myself out of going in.

There was just something so personal about going into my partner's home. I was being silly. I'd gone into Lonnie's home several times before he retired. Granted, Lonnie was saggin' and draggin' old, not like the virile, strapping Finn.

"Well?"

Finn's voice jarred me out of my head. He was standing in front of the refrigerator on the far side of the open floor family room and kitchen combo with the fridge door wide open.

"Didn't your mama tell you not to stand there with the fridge door wide open?" I asked and stalked over, trying to get ahold of myself. And lying to myself by trying to believe I was being hospitable, when I knew that if Lonnie had called me late at night, I wouldn't have gone to have a piece of his Derby pie.

"You're burning electricity." I reached around Finn, ignoring his natural scent that made my heart quicken, and went to pull out a beer.

"Seeing how Lulu pays the utilities, I'm not too concerned," he teased. "Here, let me get that for you." The touch of his fingers on mine when he gave me the beer caught me off guard and I stumbled backward and landed in the crook of his arm. "Whoa, are you okay?"

I looked up into his big brown eyes and his voice seeped into my chest, warming up my insides.

"Yes." I cleared my throat. "I guess I'm just tired." I shook my head, my hair brushing past my shoulders.

"Sit down and I'll get you a piece of that pie." He gestured to the couch. "Nice place, huh?" he called over his shoulder as he cut the pie.

"It is." I had been in here once before when I'd moved back to Cottonwood. "When I moved back, I wasn't sure if I wanted to live on Free Row even though it was my Poppa's house, so I asked Lulu to see the apartment." I rolled my eyes before I took the plate he held out. "My mama showed up while Lulu was walking me through. Mama insisted that their friendship would end if Lulu rented to me."

"Why?" Finn's lips thinned.

"Because Mama knew I didn't want to live on Free Row and that if Lulu didn't rent to me, I'd probably move back home and she'd talk me out of running for sheriff." I shook my head and put a big bite of pie on the fork and stuck it in my mouth. I closed my eyes and let the sugary treat dissolve. "Mmmm."

"I can leave you alone with the pie if you'd like." He grinned.

"I'm fine." I jabbed another big bite in my mouth. "If you forgot, we were going to have a fair hot dog tonight, so we didn't have supper."

"You're right. I'll get you another piece of pie after you finish that one."

He eased down on the couch next to me.

"My Poppa said that men like you leave small towns like ours when you get bored," I blurted out. I wished I could reel it back in, but I was feeling cornered in here.

"Your Poppa?" Finn's brows dipped, his lips flat-lined. "I thought your Poppa was no longer with us."

"He isn't, but he talked before he died." I bit the edges of my lip. I was beginning to sound crazy. "And he said that men from big cities who come to help out always get restless."

"But you're the one who suggested I become your deputy at the last town-council meeting, and when Mayor Ryland approached me tonight, you seemed to be all in." His stare made me sweat.

"It's hotter than a prostitute's doorknob on payday in here." I fanned myself and put the pie plate down.

"That is one reason I won't be leaving anytime soon." He smiled that fancy white-tooth grin. "I'm getting used to all these crazy words you string together."

"I'm sorry. I think I'm just tired." I shook my head and took a swig of the beer. "Anyways, I came here to talk about the case. So if you aren't going anywhere anytime soon, I guess we need to find a killer."

"I think you're right." He leaned back on the couch and draped his arm across the back. The grin still lingered on those lips I couldn't seem to take my eyes off of. "Tell me what you found out when you went to Owen's house."

"First off, his truck was there. I wonder how his body got into the greenhouse." I continued to tell him how I'd gotten into the trailer and would get a warrant in the morning so we could enter as we pleased just in case we got pushback from his brother. "He was married to Sandy for a long time. I'm not sure why they got divorced, but I do know that Sandy and Owen's sister-in-law didn't get along so well."

"Why not?" he asked, now much more interested in what I had to say than my nervous antics from before.

"That's the interesting part of my little visit. I stopped by to let Stanley know about his brother." I picked up the beer and took another drink. "They live on the same stretch of road and it was easy to pop over, though not easy to get answers."

His eyes narrowed. "What was his reaction?"

It was funny because we were trained to see everyone as a suspect and the empathy gene was almost always put on the back burner.

"He didn't seem too shocked. Inez, Stanley's wife, wanted to tell me something about Sandy and how she suspected Sandy wanted Owen dead because of some cookbook, but Stanley stopped her in mid-sentence. Almost threatening." I recalled the look on both of their faces. "Stanley's eyes were hooded like a hawk and when he glared at Inez, the look on her face was sheer black fright."

"Interesting." Finn looked out over the room, processing what I was saying. "You know," he nodded again, "I've seen cases like this before. The wife wants to talk, but the man doesn't. Does he hang out anywhere specific?"

"What do you mean?" I asked.

"A bar? Juke joint?" he asked.

I smiled. I never thought I'd hear the words "juke joint" come out of Finn Vincent's mouth.

"If I can find him somewhere and stall him for time, maybe you can make a visit to Inez and take her a Derby pie. Isn't that what you do when a family member dies around here? Take them food?"

"I don't make Derby pie." In fact, if it couldn't be brewed in a coffee pot or made in the microwave, then I didn't cook it.

"No, but Lulu does, and she left me another one in the refrigerator." He had a great point. "Maybe you can give your condolences as a member of society and have a nice cup of coffee over a little chat."

"I do love to chat." I smiled. "I know that he spends a lot of time at the Tractor Supply and he might go to Cole's on the river."

"River?" Finn questioned.

"The Kentucky River is not far from here. Cole's is a little shanty gambling joint where the local men like to meet up, drink beer, and shoot craps." I knew they wouldn't be comfortable with a girl around. "Maybe you can stop by in street clothes." I shrugged. "Since you are living here now, you can be one of the guys."

"I'll be sure to brush up on the game before I make an appearance. After all," he winked, "even a city slicker like me enjoys a good gamble every once in a while."

"This is good pie." I made some chit-chat, trying to make the closing of the conversation a little smoother. It was about time for me to go.

"Since I've been here, I've eaten things I'd never even heard of." He relaxed back on the couch and rested his arm on the back again, casually holding the beer on his thigh. "Have you ever been to Chicago?"

"Never." I was a little embarrassed to say that I'd only been out of Kentucky a handful of times on our family vacations to Florida.

"You don't know what you're missing. We have the best pizza." There was pure satisfaction on his face. "You're going to have to try it. That's all there is to it."

The thought of traveling with Finn to visit his hometown gave me unexpected twirls in my stomach. He made me all confused and mixed up.

"That is one thing I have missed since I joined the Reserves—good pizza." He brought the beer up to his lips and took a drink.

"I've heard how good it is." I took another sip of beer before I stood up. "I need to get going. We have an early day in the morning. I'd like to talk to Jolee about the cook-off contest and what she knew, as well as have Myrna come in to give a statement."

"Breakfast?" he asked.

"Bright and early right out there." I pointed to the door, knowing that Jolee's food truck would be parked at the curb outside of Lulu's. "The Godbeys have some family secrets they don't want uncovered." I stopped at the door and looked back. "Secrets in a small town don't stay secret for long."

Chapter Six

As soon as my head hit the pillow, I didn't open my eyes until I had hit my snooze five times. It proved to be one time too many after I got up and saw that Duke had used the bathroom next to the kitchen door.

"Poor guy." I patted my ninety-pound hound dog on top of his head. Ever since he was a puppy, I had trained him and myself to get up on the first alarm. "I can only blame myself. I'm a little tired."

I eyeballed the gift bag on the counter that my mama had given me. It was full of monogrammed towels she'd gifted me out of spite. Mama was appalled that my towels had holes in them, but even more upset that they weren't monogrammed. Everything in the woman's house was monogrammed, down to the bed linens. I knew my initials; I didn't need to keep reminding myself. But Mama had to see to it that I had some new monogrammed towels from Lulu's Boutique.

Regardless of my feelings, I reached in and grabbed a lovely purple towel with my initials monogrammed in white. Apparently not all of them were monogrammed with "No holes." There were four towels and two of each were monogrammed identically—my initials and "no holes." Mama would never know if I used one of them.

"Perfect." I let one of them fall from my fingertips and float down on the floor, covering Duke's tinkle. Duke danced around. I walked over to the back door right off the kitchen and let him run around in the fenced-in yard.

"Yoo-hoo." Speaking of Mama—her voice rang loud and clear from the back door off my kitchen. And not too long after, she was standing right in the doorway. "Kenni."

Crap. I let the screen door slam shut and hurried to grab the towel off the floor before shoving it in the cabinet underneath the sink.

"Is that my..." Mama gasped.

"Oh hi, Mama," I looked up. The pee-stained towel stuck out of the cabinet, the initial no longer white but a pale yellow. "Duke had an accident and I didn't have a quick towel."

She's going to kill me. My inner thoughts cringed in my head.

"I declare." She drew her hand to her chest. "Do you live to torture me?"

"I do no such thing, Mama." I opened the accordion doors in the kitchen that hid my washer and dryer and tossed the pee-soaked towel in the washing machine. "At least my washing machine is in here and not on the back porch like my neighbors'."

It was true. Free Row was not the best place to live in Cottonwood in these times. When Poppa lived here it was wonderful. But nowadays most people who lived on Free Row had commodity cheese and dead washers thrown in their backyards, or hell, working ones for that matter. And it wasn't unusual to walk down the sidewalk to see cars propped up on cement blocks because the tires were stolen or to get harassed by a peddler needing a handout.

Moving here was the only option I had since Mama had nixed my plans to rent Lulu's apartment—moving back in with her and Daddy was not going to happen. So here I was on Free

Row, where at least no one dared to bother the sheriff. If I did see some illegal goings on, I addressed it.

"You do, Kendrick. You do torture me." She wagged her finger at me.

"Where are you going so early, Mama?" I asked, looking at her two-piece pink chiffon suit and very modest nude heels along with a pair of white gloves.

"I had some time to kill before my meeting with the Sweet Adelines and I wanted to stop by." Mama plucked the tip of each gloved finger before she peeled them off her hand. She draped them under the handle of her bag.

"Now, Mama." I grinned. "We both know why you're here. If you think because I'm your daughter that you are going to get some inside scoop on the death of Owen Godbey, then you can take your fancy self right on out that door and keep going."

"Kendrick, you are awful. Just awful," she cried. "None of your friends treat their mamas the way you treat me." She lifted her chin in the air and looked down her nose at me. "I know because we talk about our children."

"What do you say about me?" I checked the time on my phone that was plugged in on the counter.

"I tell them how proud I am of you." She sucked in a deep breath. "I mean, you could fancy up your sheriff's outfit a bit, but you uphold the law and keep our precious town safe."

"Thank you, Mama." I walked over and hugged her. "Now, I want to keep making you proud, so I have to go get ready. I'm meeting Finn at the food truck for breakfast."

"Breakfast?" She sounded happy. "Honey, I've got the best breakfast casserole—you can make it and have him over. That hunk will never leave."

"I've done told you more than once that Finn and I are strictly coworkers," I called on my way back down the hall toward my room.

"Just think about it. That hunky man could become my son-in-law sheriff and you can stay home." The excitement dripped from her voice at the thought. "Finally get you out of this dangerous job."

I had no idea what fantasy world Mama was living in, but I had to put a stop to it right now before anyone else got a whiff of her silly notion. How was I going to do that? I wondered as I opened my closet door and took out one of my many brown sheriff's shirts and brown pants. It was pretty great not having to worry about what I was going to wear to work every day.

"Mama, don't be getting no ideas. Besides, I'm sheriff." After I got dressed, I tucked the edges of my brown shirt into my brown pants and stuck my Poppa's pin right beneath my five-point sheriff's badge. "Finn is not going to be sheriff and we are only coworkers."

I grabbed a ponytail holder and walked back down the hall, pulling up my hair snug in the holder. I'd gotten pretty good at just throwing on clothes and going.

"At least put on some lipstick," Mama snarled. "The least you could do."

"Mama, what time is your meeting?" I recalled Poppa saying something about Sandy Godbey being a Sweet Adeline.

"Why? Are you finally going to show off your talented voice?" Another one of Mama's la-la-land ideas. She was sure I was destined for greatness all my younger years and put me in the church choir, but she didn't get a clue when the song director continually stuck me in the back behind all the tall people.

"I have a few questions I need answered, and I know that I can always count on your group of friends," I said.

"Today we are having a luncheon to celebrate some ten-year anniversaries." She nudged me with her elbow. "I'm in charge, so you come on. It's a good day for you to come so you can see what a difference Adelines make in our community. Besides, it's at Kim's Buffet and you can eat." Her eyes sliding around my kitchen was her silent way of noticing how I didn't cook.

Another thing about Mama—she was always trying to fatten me up.

"That sounds good." My mouth watered thinking about the delicious Chinese food. "I'll see you soon."

I ushered Mama out the door and grabbed my walkie-talkie, strapping it on my shoulder.

"Come on." I patted my leg for Duke to come. He loved going to Jolee's and grabbing a biscuit or two, and then I could leave him at the office where he would sleep the day away. Or he could ride around with me as I ran back to Owen's trailer to check out things in the daylight, which reminded me to get a warrant.

I pushed the button on the walkie-talkie. "Betty."

"Yes, Kenni," she answered immediately.

"I need you to get me a warrant for Owen Godbey's property that includes the house, land, and the truck." I pulled up to the curb in front of On The Run, Jolee's food truck. "Just in case we get pushback from anyone, we have it."

Finn was already there.

"Will do, Kenni." Betty clicked off.

"Two Sunny Goose Sammies," Jolee hollered over her shoulder after she saw me and Finn walking up. "Coming up."

She looked between us and smiled. Duke scratched at the side door on the food truck because he knew Jolee would throw him a biscuit. And she did.

"Who are you talking to?" I curled up on my tiptoes and looked in the small window of the food truck.

"Her." Jolee shook her head and rolled her eyes.

I poked my head inside the food-truck window and was

surprised to see Viola White standing there in her five-foot-four yellow-pantsuit-clad glory with a real fox stole fastened around her shoulders. Her hair was tucked under a hairnet and the food gloves had big humps from where I knew Viola had on her signature rings. She was rolling out the dough for the famous biscuits.

Viola was a force. She owned White's Jewelry on Main Street and was by far the richest woman in Cottonwood. But what Myrna had said about Viola being in the cook-off with her and Owen must've been right. Still, I found myself shocked, which was not easy to do. I'd seen it all now.

Viola's eyes magnified under her black-rimmed glasses. "Don't be lollygagging around the window here. Move along."

"Oh, we ain't lollygagging, Ms. Viola." Finn stepped up and did his best southern accent. "We are dilly-dallying." He winked.

"You just might fit in here after all, Yank." She smiled back at him before she grabbed the steel round dough cutter and plopped out biscuits on a cookie sheet.

I swear I rolled my eyes so hard I saw my own brain. If the shoe were on my foot and I'd said that to her, she'd have called my mama despite the fact that I was a twenty-eight-year-old woman.

Jolee chomped on her gum and smiled, making the freckles across her nose widen. Her blonde hair was braided in her signature pigtails that hung down on each side of her head. She'd said it was easy to do and it kept her hair out of the way.

"Do you have a minute to talk?" I asked.

"Viola, here is your chance." Jolee untied the apron from around her waist and pulled the string over top her head.

"Don't you worry. I've got this." Viola grabbed the apron and hip bumped Jolee right out of the way.

I met Jolee on the side of the food truck where Duke was still sitting, begging for more.

"She's got this." I laughed, trying my best Viola impression, knowing that she was used to being waited on, not the other way around.

"She don't got that." Jolee pointed to the long line of customers that were there to get breakfast on the run. "Is this about Owen Godbey?" she asked, looking between the two of us. "Because everyone is talking about it."

"Sort of." I started my line of questioning while Finn and Duke waited at the counter for our food to come out. "What on Earth is this cook-off about?"

"A little fun-hearted competition between me and Ben Harrison." She smirked.

"It's fun-hearted until you lose. Or vice versa." I pointed out. "Regardless, tell me how you picked the three candidates."

"I was just as shocked as you when I saw Viola White walk in to fill out an application. I figured the applicants would be younger folks, but they weren't. And when Owen came to fill out an application, I knew I had to have him." She shrugged.

"Why?" I asked, wondering what appeal Owen would have to her.

"His mama's okra recipe," she said, like it was something I should've known about. "Everyone has tried to get their hands on it for years. And it was rumored that he was willed her cookbook. So naturally when he came in I knew I had to get him to make it."

"Did he?" I asked.

"Not now. The rule Ben and I came up with was we each got three candidates. Over the past week we've been having them help us in our environments. Mine being the truck. But you've been with Finn...I mean, you've been so busy lately that I haven't really seen you." Her slip up was no slip up. Finn had everyone talking in Cottonwood, and not about his professional abilities. "Anyways," she glossed over her words just so I knew it was a dig at me, "I really did pick the best three I felt were right for my team. Then by the end of two weeks, which is this week, I'll pick the best out of my three, two now, and the best one goes up against Ben's best one. We're having a cook-off between the two at the fairgrounds. Doolittle Bowman already approved it."

Doolittle had two jobs in Cottonwood, which wasn't uncommon in a small town like ours. She was the town-council president as well as the county clerk.

"What does the winner get out of it?" There had to be some sort of value in order for her three candidates to enter. I mean, Viola was already über wealthy and had her own store. Same with Myrna. "Why would any three of your candidates want to do this?"

"I don't know. Money. Legacy." She'd said something that caught my attention.

"They all have money," I said, but then remembered that I'd heard Owen was in need of some money for his medication.

"Right, but when do you have enough? See, each person will sell me their recipe and they will get their name on the menu, along with licensing fees each month of the total sale of their food item." She definitely had an interesting and enticing prize.

Of course, I'd heard all this from Myrna, but I'd much rather hear it with my own ears from the source.

"So they only had to invest in this for two weeks and that's it. They get paid each month." It was very cut and dry.

"Yep." She folded her arms in front of her. "Now that Owen is," she stuck her tongue out and rolled her eyes up in her head, "it doesn't look like I'm even going to get to look at that recipe. But the upside is that I don't have to listen to Owen and Myrna fuss and fight about her firing him." She curled her lips in. "Still," she shook her head, the edges of her lips dipped down, "I still can't believe he's dead. He really didn't bother nobody."

"No, he didn't," I said, but I wanted to get back the firing thing. "She fired him?" There was a tidbit of information Myrna had left out last night.

"Yep. A few days ago." She cocked her head to the side. "Didn't you know?"

"No." This didn't look good for Myrna. "Who told you?" I couldn't help but think it was a little suspicious on Myrna's part that she left that out. Though she did stumble for words when I'd questioned her last night.

"Myrna and Owen. Both." She shrugged. "They both talked bad about each other when we first started the contest. Ben and I got all the contestants together and explained the competition and rules."

"You hungry?" Finn walked up holding two cardboard cartons. "Our coffee is up there. I thought you could grab those while I grab a seat."

"We don't have time to eat here." I turned back to Jolee. "Can you watch Duke for me? During your deliveries for Meals on Wheels, you can drop him off at the office."

"Aye, aye." She saluted and trotted off back toward the truck, where I was sure Viola had just fired her own self.

"I'm done with these people," Viola belted out the window with her fist in the air, her bracelets jingling all the way up her arm. She untied her apron, balled it up, and threw it on the ground. "To hell with you all."

She and Jolee had a few words before Viola stormed off. I guessed Myrna was Jolee's winner by default now.

"What was that about?" I asked Finn after grabbing the coffees, heading toward the Wagoneer.

"Viola was giving everyone some sort of hash brown breakfast." He held up the food. "Even us." He laughed. "No matter what you ordered, when she was working alone, you got the same thing. This. I'm not complaining because I'm hungry. Everyone else fussed and made her mad."

"We can't worry about this. We've got bigger fish to fry, like Myrna Savage and her big fat secret," I muttered.

"What's that?" Finn stopped shy of the Jeep and looked at me.

"According to Jolee, Myrna fired Owen, and if you recall, she told us last night that he wouldn't be there because it was late, not because he didn't work for her anymore." The words stung my throat as they came out.

Myrna Savage was about to get a house call.

Chapter Seven

Finn walked around to the back of Myrna's house while I knocked on the front. The Petal Pusher's delivery van was parked where it had been last night, but Myrna wasn't answering the door.

"She's in the greenhouse." Finn poked his head around the side of the house.

"You've got to be kidding me." My jaw dropped. Did no one have respect for the law? I let out a deep sigh and walked around to the back of the house.

There she was, in the greenhouse with the door wide open, music spilling out. The police tape had been ripped in half.

"She doesn't seem to listen very well." Finn shook his head. "I'm glad I got what I needed last night."

The wet morning dew was sprinkled all over the lush green lawn like little teardrops and the smell of freshly stem-cut flowers flowed out of the greenhouse along with a happy humming tune.

"Myrna," I scolded. "What are you doing in here?"

She turned, a pair of pliers in her grip. "Kendrick Lowry, you almost gave me a heart attack." She pulled the pliers to her chest. "Then who would do my funeral flowers?"

"I'm not joking." I stood with my legs apart and my hands rested on my sheriff's belt to show her how serious I was. "This is a crime scene. And you could go to jail for tampering with evidence."

"According to Betty Murphy, that fine young man already had the evidence put in baggies and sent off to the lab." She turned back to the floral arrangement she was working on and snipped a few stems before placing it in the milk-glass vase. "Not to mention I had floods of orders coming in for poor old Owen's layout."

"You mean to tell me that people have already called this early?" I checked the time on my cell.

"Honey, death waits for no one, and neither do these flowers." She pulled some baby's breath from the freezer. The door slammed shut and fog crept up along the glass. I shivered. "Everyone knows that I only keep a certain amount of each flower and if they call too late, then they are shit out of luck. That's the way it is. Not to mention competing on who is going to order the biggest."

"The biggest?" Finn questioned.

"Oh honey, like the repast where people cook their best recipe, the bigger the arrangement, the higher on the social ladder you are. Right now, Ruby Smith is winning." She winked and tapped an order form in front of her with the tip of the pliers.

It wasn't unusual that Ruby had bought the biggest arrangement to be sent. It made perfect sense since Poppa had told me Rae Lynn and Ruby were best friends. I was still planning on paying her a visit.

The greenhouse phone rang and Myrna quickly picked it up. "Petal Pushers, Myrna Savage, floral extraordinaire, at your service."

"Extraordinaire?" Finn whispered, an eyebrow raised.

Myrna gave us the shoulder and hunched over the receiver of the phone. She gave the person on the other end of the line a few *uh-huhs*, *mmms*, and *yeps* before she turned back around. She gave us the sweet smile as she hung the phone up.

"Why didn't you tell me that you fired Owen Godbey?" I asked, hoping the surprise question would catch her off guard.

Myrna's body stiffened. Slowly she laid the pliers down on the counter and sucked in a deep breath.

"It wasn't that I thought you weren't going to find out." Her southern accent deepened. "I wanted to call Wally Lamb before you hauled me off to jail on some suspicion. I watch all them cop shows and I see how this all works, Kenni."

She referred to Wally Lamb, the local lawyer.

"Sheriff," I corrected her. If there was one thing that bugged me being the sheriff in my own town was the fact they didn't call me by my title. It might have seemed petty. But during official business, I felt it was a lack of respect.

"Sheriff then." Her eyes drew down me and back up. "Whatever." She stuck her hands out in front of her, wrists bent, fingers dangling down. "Arrest me for something I didn't do."

"Then answer the question." What part did she not understand? "If you have nothing to hide, then why didn't you tell me? For all I know, you had a good reason."

"You mean the fact that he tried to steal my garden-growing recipe right out from under my nose?" Myrna reached for a felted cigar box on the sill of the window. She opened it and took out a stack of index cards. She thumbed through them and pulled one out, pushing it toward me. "This here is my aunt's recipe box she made. It was the only thing she left me in her will. It seemed silly to everyone in our family, but it's priceless to me. My aunt was a master garden grower. She had the most beautiful garden and landscaped yard you'd have ever laid your eyes upon. She could make a weed look like a fresh summer rose. She told me, 'Myrna, you've got the gift like me.' So when she died, I got this box and all its contents. My family laughed because they got all her worldly belongings and now they are poor as field mice. Not me." She pulled the index card to her chest and hugged it. "She gave me the gift of everlasting life. Her secret growing recipe." Her voice deepened. "Owen Godbey was out here trying to steal it. I fired him on the spot." She took the cards and put them back in the box, slamming down the lid. "I didn't kill Owen Godbey. Even though I wanted to."

"Why would he want your recipe?" Finn asked.

"He wanted my secret grow recipe to use on his okra garden. He said the soil on his property was no good and Stanley wouldn't let him use their property to continue to grow the okra garden Rae Lynn had already started." She picked the pliers up. She snipped so hard and fast at the flowers, Finn and I had to watch for flying pieces. "The only thing I could reckon was that he wanted to win the cook-off so bad that he would go to any lengths to steal. After all, I did hear that he was in financial need for his medicine. Now, that's just hearsay."

"You caught him trying to steal your recipe?" I wanted to clarify.

"No, but why else was he here?" she assumed.

I couldn't take hearsay for truth, but it was definitely something I could check into.

"Do you know what medicine he was taking?" I questioned.

"Oh, I don't know. It wasn't like I was married to the man." She pish-poshed me. "He was gimping around here anyways. Complaining about ailments and aches. So he wasn't going to last delivering for me much longer because I have a lot of hospital deliveries, and with the floral show coming up, he wasn't about to help out with that." She glanced over at Finn. A smile crept up on her face. "I need a strapping young man for that."

"What hurt him?" I asked, bringing her lusty eyes back in focus.

"I don't know. He complained about his back, his knees, his legs, even his hair follicles. He complained like an old lady." She tsked and pulled some yellow roses out of the refrigerator. "Now, can you please rip down all this crime-scene tape so I can get back to work? Or cuff me?"

"No one is cuffing anyone." Wally Lamb stood at the door of the greenhouse. He was as shady as they came—his nickname in high school was Low-down Lamb. He did sneaky things to win school elections. "You are looking mighty fine, Kenni." Wally slid past me, his head turning all angles so he could get a good look at me. "Love a woman in a uniform." He grinned. "You ever decide on my offer?"

"Sheriff Lowry." Finn stepped up as my nose curled up in disgust.

"Oh, you have a talking puppet now, Kenni?" Wally asked, his eyes focused on me. He winked. "I always said I'd be your deputy."

Wally wore a black three-piece suit and shiny black shoes. I heard he kept the Cottonwood Laundromat in business with all of his fancy clothes. It was rumored that he even worked out in suits. His blond hair was always combed straight back with product in it. Tina, from Tiny Tina's salon, said that he bought cases of that stuff a month. I'd believe it. I'd also heard that he spent a lot of time at the Lancôme counter at the mall. Now that was just a rumor.

"Listen, buddy." Finn's chest poked out.

"It's okay." I put my hand out on Finn's chest and inwardly giggled at the muscles tickling my palm. "This is Wally Lamb. He's a local attorney who I grew up with."

"She's a feisty one." Wally winked again. A toothpick jogged up and down from the corner of his mouth. "I was just at Cowboy's Catfish to see you, but Betty said you weren't in yet. I took my chances and here you are." He turned his attention to

Myrna. "These fine law-abiding Cottonwood officers aren't keeping you from your job, are they, Miss Myrna?"

"Don't be sassy, Wally," Myrna warned. "I can hold my own. And I already told them that I fired Owen Godbey because I caught him trying to steal from me."

"Does that appease you?" Wally asked, plucking one of the roses from the bundle. He brought it up to his nose and took a nice long whiff. I was having a hard time hiding my distaste for his smarmy ways.

"What would appease me, Wally, is for you to get your client out and have her stay out of a crime scene like I told her to last night." I adjusted my stance, straight back, hands clasped in front of me, and stared directly at Wally. "I sure wouldn't want to have to call the Attorney General and let him know that a certain lawyer isn't following the law, because you and I both know that your client isn't."

"But my—" Myrna started to protest before Wally bent down and whispered something in her ear.

Her chin and eyes lifted.

"She's going to take her orders with her and find a florist to help her until this is cleared up." Wally gestured around the greenhouse.

"Fine." I lifted my hands.

"Do you mind if I take a look around your house?" Finn asked Myrna when she and Wally walked past him.

"I don't see why not." Myrna crossed her arms. When Wally started to say something, she put her hand up to stop him. "I have nothing to hide."

"Myrna, we will be in touch. Finn, you go look around while I put up the police tape again." I picked the tape up off the floor that Myrna had easily ignored and stepped all over.

"My offer still stands, Kenni." Wally stopped at the greenhouse door and held the rose out for me to take. The smile on his face made me nauseous. "Me and you would make one helluva team." His words strung together. "Put that rose on my tab," he said to Myrna. She snickered as I reluctantly took the flower.

"Myrna, we will be in touch." I said. "Wally, be sure your client stays in Cottonwood."

The greenhouse door slammed behind them.

"Who on Earth does he think he is?" Finn snarled and jerked the tape taut.

"It's Wally." My voice was flat along with my eyes. The inside looked secure, so I gestured Finn to follow me outside. "Wally Lamb is a wannabe big-city lawyer. He isn't even the county attorney; he got beat in a landslide last election. I have to pick what battles I want to fight and the ones I don't. Wally is not a threat."

Though I'd heard another rumor that he was going to run again next election, which was when my term was up. The very people who elected you could turn on you in a minute. I'd seen it.

"We can't be bothered with Wally." I kind of liked how Finn took up for me. If Lonnie was still my deputy, he wouldn't have even been able to hear what was said. "Besides, he's harmless. Just a good ole boy."

"Well, I don't like him." Finn looked back in the greenhouse. He jerked the yellow rose Wally had given me out of my hand and threw it on the ground on our way back to the house. Not only did he step on it, he twisted his foot, smashing the petals in the dewy grass.

Chapter Eight

"You can't let Wally Lamb get under your skin," Betty Murphy quipped from her desk in the office after Finn continued to fuss about good southern gentleman and how disrespectful Wally was to the sheriff, never mind a woman. "I'm glad you didn't find no evidence in Myrna's house. I do like her."

Wally Lamb had decided to follow Finn around the house and let me be. Finn had taken one part of the house and I looked around the other. There was nothing but flower magazines, flower equipment, and moth balls around Myrna's house. There wasn't a sign of any barbwire. Everything I had on Myrna was circumstantial and had to do with her firing Owen because she caught him red-handed trying to steal from her.

"Wally was disrespectful to Kenni," Finn told her.

"Don't you worry about Kenni." Betty laughed. "She can defend herself, right?"

"Yep," I said.

"I know you can, but he needed to be put in his place. Unless..." His voice trailed off.

"Unless what?" My eyes narrowed in anticipation.

"Unless you do want to go out with him." Finn shrugged.

"Please." I rolled my eyes. Betty squealed with laughter, causing Finn to laugh.

"Well, he did get under my skin." Finn shook his head.

Duke walked over to Finn's desk, where he kept treats for my loyal companion. Finn held a treat out and Duke sat so still. "Shhhh." He put the treat on the edge of the desk and Duke didn't move, his eyes on the prize. "I've been training him to stay with the temptation right there. It's something the dogs in the reserve learned to do and I always thought it was so cool." He looked over at Betty. "Maybe I can teach him to attack Wally Lamb."

Betty giggled like a schoolgirl at Finn's joke that I didn't find funny. I did find it odd that Duke wasn't moving the least tiniest bit. Betty and I watched Finn finally give poor Duke the okay to eat the treat.

The smell of fried bologna crept up from under the door of Cowboy's Catfish and sent my insides to growling. That was one problem with having the office attached to the greasy spoon. Since Cottonwood was so small, there was never a need to have a big jail or even a big office, so the town council had rented the back space from Bartleby Fry, the owner of the building and of Cowboy's. The one-cell, three-desk space had been enough up until recently. I'd been finding the space had become a little too tight.

"It must be bologna day." I inhaled and let out a big exhale. "Duke will have his nose stuck under the door all day. He's a sucker for bologna and so am I. Too bad I'm going to the Sweet Adeline luncheon."

"Yeah, ever since Jolee dropped him by, he's been wandering over there a time or two," Betty pointed out. "Doolittle Bowman called to remind you of the council meeting tomorrow night." She lifted a paper in the air. "Here's your warrant."

"Thanks, Betty." I walked over and took it out of her hand. The judge had given me the full warrant.

"I'm going to the town meeting." Finn stood by the fax

machine, checking out the pages that had come from the lab. "Are you going to propose the new office space?"

"Eh?" The corner of Betty's lips snarled. "What did you say?"

"We will be at the meeting," I said a little louder, a smile on my face as I sat at my desk and typed my notes from my visit with Myrna this morning on my computer. Everything had to be documented, even the smashed rose.

"Who what?" Betty's false teeth clacked. She stuck her finger in her ear to adjust her hearing aids. "Darn things're already going bad and I paid a lot for them."

Finn walked over to Betty's desk and looked down at the earpieces he'd wrongly thought would be a good idea to replace my old Velcro walkie-talkie and picked them up.

"This is why your ears aren't working." He held up Betty's hearing aids. "You've got the wrong earpiece in."

Shock and awe swept across Betty's face. All of us snorted out in laughter.

"I told you those earpieces weren't going to work." Gently I rubbed my walkie-talkie that was velcroed on my shoulder. "This works just fine and we have another one in the closet over there for you."

He simply shook his head.

"Any messages from Max?" I asked Betty after she'd gotten herself situated.

"He said Stanley came by and identified the body early this morning." Betty held the piece of paper up to her eyes and continued to read. "They are going to have him cremated. Services will be held as soon as the body is cleared and there will only be a memorial. No funeral. No preacher. No repast."

"Well, that is going to ding-dong the auxiliary women." It was a bit of news I could take to them. "Myrna was already filling flower orders."

"Speaking of repast." Finn walked over to the closet and pulled out the tangled-up walkie-talkie that used to be Lonnie's. "Don't forget that you said you'd stop by Inez's with that pie. Did you find out anything about Cole's?"

"I didn't, but I'll get on that too." I stood up to go into Cowboy's. All the men in the community would probably be gathering for lunch about now, and if there was something going on at Cole's, they'd know. If not, Finn could still go on over to the Tractor Supply and poke around. "I'm heading across the street to Kim's Buffet, but I'll walk through Cowboy's. I'll see if Bartleby knows anything about Cole's and give you a shout." I turned one last time to Finn. "Do me a favor when you head over to Tractor Supply and ask around about the electric barbwire and if anyone has purchased any. After that, can you run out to Owen's trailer and look for any cookbooks you see?" Then I glanced back at Betty. "Get Finn a copy of the warrant so he can have one with him, and see what you can find out about Sandy Godbey and where I might find her."

"Sure thing, Sheriff." Betty quickly turned and picked up the phone. "And Sheriff..." Betty stopped me. She put the receiver of the phone under her chin. "Rowdy called and said that some flowers had been stolen from graves and he wanted to make a report. He said it wasn't urgent and he wasn't going to be there the rest of the day, so stop by tomorrow if you can."

"Okay. I'll catch up with him." I pushed the door open between the kitchen of Cowboy's Catfish and the office.

"Mornin', Sheriff." Bartleby held up a greasy spatula when I walked past. "I sure hated to hear about Owen. I guess Myrna did more than fire him."

"Don't be going and pointing fingers. We don't know exactly how Owen died." I eyed the sizzling bologna in the cast-iron skillet. My mouth salivated. "Why do you think Myrna did it?"

"The legend of the cookbook." He wiggled his brows. "Everyone in the county wants a look at the infamous book."

That was about the fourth person who said something about Rae Lynn's cookbook. What was so special about that okra recipe? There was one thing for sure: I needed to get my hands on it.

"What's so important about a cookbook?" I asked.

"Rae Lynn has the best okra around and she claimed the secret was safe in her recipe book." He scrunched his face and his eyebrows rose. "I wouldn't mind taking a gander at it."

"Anyways, I know that you see Stanley at Cole's. How is he holding up?" I asked, poking around.

"He didn't come to Cole's last night, but we've got some beer drinkin' to do tonight in honor of Owen. Among other things." There was a hint of secrets on his face. "I left a message with Inez for him to stop by tonight."

"You mean gambling tonight?" I asked, followed up with a laugh. "Everyone in town knows what is going down at Cole's."

"What?" Bartleby asked in an offended tone. "Why, nothin' is going down. We are hard-working men who enjoy a drink or three."

"I hear ya."

I waved.

"You ain't staying for my Kentucky round steak?" he asked, using the fancy name we called fried bologna.

"I wish I could," I hollered over my shoulder. "But I've been invited to the Sweet Adelines."

"And you're starting to think about election time." A knowing grin crept up on his lips because he knew that the election was two years away, and it was about the time everyone started to talk about it. "I guess you'll be turning up at all sorts of events in the near future."

"I reckon I will," I called out over my shoulder and headed

out of the kitchen into the dining room, where the restaurant was filled.

Yep, secrets in a small town didn't stay covered up for long. I couldn't help but wonder if Myrna's story about Owen trying to steal her recipe wasn't really the other way around.

Chapter Nine

I greeted, nodded, waved, and shook hands as I made my way out onto Main Street.

It was nice to see a few days where the sun was out. We'd had an unseasonable amount of rain over the past few months and everything was finally drying out. Old historic buildings lined Main Street on both sides. A few people were gathered around the town troubadour as he strung his guitar and twanged the songs of old country crooners like Conway Twitty. The hanging baskets on the carriage lights were freshly made, thanks to Myrna Savage.

The traffic whizzed by and my thoughts got lost in the sound. Myrna did a lot for this community. She was the only florist. She was the president of the Beautification Committee. She sat on the town council and she was bound and determined to win that cook-off. Was she really after Owen's secret recipe in his book?

Or had Owen tried to lift her grow recipe like she'd said, and made her mad enough to murder him?

"Anything is possible." Poppa stood next to me on the curb.

"You can read my thoughts?" I whispered.

"No, that would be neat though." He huffed and puffed

alongside me across the street. "I can tell by the look on your face that you haven't ruled out Myrna Savage."

I nodded slightly so it wouldn't look as if I had a tic or something going on with my neck.

Kim's Buffet was packed with older women in pillbox hats, gloves, and matching pink suits like the one Mama had on this morning. The tables were decorated with pink tablecloths, pink doilies for each place setting, and pink glitter. When I looked around, Poppa was gone.

"Welcome to the luncheon," Mrs. Kim said in her accented English. She gestured me to move along. I had to do a double take when I noticed it was her under the sea of pink. "What?" she scowled.

"I'm happy to be here."

I moved along and noticed my mama in the far right corner, so I went far left.

"Why, Kendrick." Ruby Smith waved and headed in my direction. "I'm so glad to see you. Your mama said you've been spending many long hours with that new deputy." She winked, her shoulders bunched up around her ears. She shifted her tall, lanky body to the right, one arm curled around her waist, the other in the air flailing a cocktail around. "You know what I say," she used her fingertips to brush down the edges of her short red hair, "'let the man take you to bed and enjoy all if it.'" The words oozing out of her orange-painted lips were like poison to my ears.

"That's some advice I won't be taking. He's my deputy and I'm the sheriff," I reminded her.

"Oh, honey, I know, but a little pretend play never hurt a soul." She lifted her glass to her lips and swigged it back. "Now, where is that boy with the drinks?" Her head rotated around.

"He's as professional as I am. We have a working relationship and that's all." How did this get turned around on me? This was exactly how gossip around here got started. "I need to come to the store and get me a new clock."

"Oh, no." Her brows formed a V. "Dick and Bob died?"

I'd gotten the mantel anniversary clock from her antique store when I moved onto Free Row. The gold plaque that was screwed on the front of it said "Happy Anniversary Dick and Bob."

"No. Dick and Bob are as happy as ever and about to have yet another anniversary." I knew that only because I'd moved on Free Row once I was running for sheriff. "I need a clock for my kitchen and I was going to come down and look around."

Plus I wanted to talk to her about Rae Lynn and that cookbook since I'd understood them to be best friends. Here wasn't the place.

"You come on by tomorrow. I'll fix you up. I got this cute cat one whose eyes roll around and has this long black tail that swings back and forth." She grabbed another cocktail from the tray when the boy passed.

"Being here reminds me of Sandy Godbey." I pinched my lips and shook my head, hoping to score a little information.

"If she was still a member, which she is not." Ruby waved her hand around. The cocktail swished side to side. "I'd run her off. I hope Rae Lynn is haunting her."

"Why?" I asked and took an eggroll off the food tray when it passed.

"She always said that girl wasn't a gold digger, but an ingredient digger." Ruby snickered. "Who ever heard the like? Ingredient digger."

"What is that?" I played coy.

"According to Rae Lynn, all Sandy wanted or talked about was the cookbook. And that is what started the family feud." Ruby got interrupted as the Sweet Adelines started to sing and bring the celebration to order.

"Family feud?" I asked. "I thought those two were thicker than thieves." I referred to the brothers.

"Only when Rae Lynn was living. God bless her soul." Ruby's lips thinned. She bowed her head and said a prayer. "I reckon she was standing at them pearly gates Preacher always talks about. You know." Her eyes drew to mine. "The one where Peter is supposed to be with open arms?"

"I'm sure she was." I gave a sympathetic eye her way. Both of us turned to the harmonizing Adelines that had taken their place in the windows at the front of the restaurant.

"I'd gone down to Wally Lamb's to redo some business stuff and I was sitting in the waiting room until my appointment. I couldn't help but hear Rae Lynn in his office discussing her will," Ruby said.

"You heard her talk about her will?" I asked, baiting Ruby for more information.

"Thin walls." Her jaw locked.

"Yes, I bet they are in that new strip mall." It sure would be nice to hear what she knew, even though I knew I was going to have to get Wally Lamb to give me a look at the will. "What did you hear Rae Lynn say?" I acted as if I was just being nosy and not on the job.

"She told Wally Lamb to give Stanley the land and house." She sucked in a deep breath. "She only gave Owen that darn cookbook." She shook her head. "Poor Owen."

The Sweet Adelines sang their hearts out, filling the restaurant with their music, making it hard for me to continue having a conversation with Ruby.

Mama stood in the middle. Her mouth opened wide with the corners tipped up as she sang the songs alongside her friends. Her head swayed like a wave to the tune of their voices. Her eyes lit up and her smile grew bigger when she saw me standing in the back.

"Sheriff." Edna Easterly moseyed up to me and greeted me in her slow southern voice. She might've been a Sweet Adeline, but I heard she wouldn't get all fancied up in a pink suit like the others.

I'd heard right.

"Now, Edna." I looked up at her brown fedora with the pink ribbon tied around the base. A long pink feather was hot-glued to the ribbon and curled over the top of the hat. On the opposite side was a notecard with the word "Reporter" written in pink Sharpie to match. She wore a pair of brown khaki pants, a brown tee, and pink Converse lace-ups that had seen much better days. "Is this the latest Sweet Adeline attire?" I smiled.

The edges of her eyes softened and lifted when she returned the gesture.

"You know me. I've always got to be ready when there might be a story around. I told them that I wasn't going to be putting on a suit for no one." She retrieved a little notebook out of her pocket and pulled a pen from behind her ear. She turned her head toward the sweet sounds of her friends and asked, "Is there a reason you're here? Any leads on Owen Godbey?"

"I'm here to support my mama." I nodded toward the singing group. Mama's face beamed.

"I can smell a lead a mile away." Edna's eyes glazed over. "You, Sheriff, are here to find a lead."

"I'll tell you what." I was about to make a deal that Edna couldn't refuse. "I could ask around here and get some details about a particular Sweet Adeline. Or I could give you the exclusive to run the story before anyone else after it's solved."

"I'm listening." She nodded her head toward the door and her body followed.

I headed outside with her. She started to write in the notepad as I spoke.

"I know that you have your ear and finger on the hot

button." I wasn't above stroking Edna's ego. "I also know that you give a fair and balanced account of all the women in Cottonwood, and Sandy Godbey would be no exception."

"Are you telling me that Sandy is a suspect?" Edna asked.

"Everyone is a suspect, Edna. This is where I need you." My eyes shifted to the notepad and back up to her face. "I need you to help me find her. There's no listed address, nothing in the courthouse documents from their divorce. I'd just like to have a word with her. Anyone who knew him."

"Stanley and Inez put a notice in the paper. I was a little shocked they aren't having a funeral." Curiosity set on her face.

"They will have to have a service without his remains."

There was a twinkle in her eyes. "I'm sure I can locate her. She was a fascinating woman." Edna scribbled a few things on her notepad.

"How?"

I wanted to know any particulars I could get.

"She and Owen were tied at the hip. I think it was a shock to him when she filed for divorce. In fact, I got a copy of the papers and she wanted the family cookbook and that was all. When Owen wouldn't hand it over, she sued him for everything." Edna paused and glanced out over Main Street.

That darn cookbook again.

Betty Murphy chirped over the walkie-talkie, "Calling Sheriff Lowry, calling Sheriff Lowry." I slid my finger along the volume button to turn it down.

"Hold that thought." I held up my finger to Edna and took a few steps away for privacy. I pushed in the button on the side. "Go ahead, Betty."

"Max Bogus called and he said he needs to see you right away. Urgent." I barely let Betty finish before I ran across Main Street and around Cowboy's Catfish, where I'd parked the Jeep in the alley behind it.

"Tell him I'm on my way." I jumped in and put the Jeep in gear. "I'll call you later, Edna!" I hollered out the window.

"Wait. Is something going on?" Edna ran after me. I didn't answer.

"I'll say," Betty quipped back. "Max said he had the cause of death and you might be surprised. Poison."

"Poison?" I pushed the pedal as far as it could go.

Chapter Ten

The Jeep nearly jumped the curb as it skidded up in front of Cottonwood Funeral Home. I couldn't wait to see what Max had gotten from the preliminary report.

"I remember being laid right there in that window." Poppa's ghost appeared in the passenger side of the Jeep. "It was in my will."

"I remember." I gulped down the lump in my throat that always lodged there when I recalled that terrible day. "Where have you been?"

I was good at changing the subject when it came to matters I didn't want to discuss.

"I've been looking around." He was sneaking around in his cool ghost form. "But I think you are going to have to find that cookbook to see what everyone is talking about."

"Tell me something I don't know." I was already exhausted and the day wasn't nearly over.

"I'm working on that." He grinned as though he had something up his sleeve. "Give me your thoughts."

"All the signs point to Myrna, but it doesn't feel like she did it. In fact, there is no way she'd have the strength to hog-tie his ankles around an active electric fence." I tapped the wheel with my fingers.

"If he was already passed out, then she could've rolled him." He shrugged.

"Max did tell Betty that he found some poison. That's why we're here," I said.

"Poison?" Poppa's brows furrowed.

"Someone had to have poisoned him first, then tied him up, which could've been Myrna." I took the keys out of the ignition and grabbed my bag off the floorboard. "Let's go."

Poppa and I walked up to the old house that had been transformed into the funeral home, just like most businesses in Cottonwood. The two-story brick home had fifteen-foot ceilings, along with rich crown moldings, large door frames, and hardwood floors that made it a perfect funeral home. Creepiness exuded in there. Not to mention how the basement had completely been remodeled into a morgue equipped with all the latest technology, including quick lab results.

Max had on his usual blue lab coat, big goggles, and scalpel in hand and stood over Owen.

"Kenni." He waved me over. The scalpel clinked when he placed it on the metal table. "I'm preparing Owen for cremation. The autopsy report is on the counter over there with your name on it."

"Betty said something about a poisoning?" I asked, walking over to the counter and picking up the manila envelope.

"I think that's what killed him. I definitely rule this a homicide, though we already thought that." He continued to finish up on Owen. "It's going to take a few days, maybe weeks to get back all the results, but I've seen it before and it looks like a poisoning by antifreeze. It's practically tasteless and can be disguised in liquids, food, really anything."

"Now it's official." I sighed, knowing that now I had to handle the information I was collecting in a different way. "And anything Myrna Savage told me is going on the record."

Luckily I had learned to read Max's bad handwriting and looked in the Marks and Wound section.

"Postmortem ankle wounds," I noted. "Probable cause of death, poison ingestion."

He also wrote in the report how he thought Owen had probably ingested some antifreeze that was disguised by the drink he'd had in his empty stomach.

Farther down, the "homicide" box was checked, making this an official murder investigation.

"That means that the poison killed him and they likely wanted to cover it up by using the barbwire." Poppa looked over my shoulder. "Whoever did this thinks you are going to look for whoever owns that particular barbwire. Definitely post-mortem, and the poison killed him." Max waved me over again. "Look here." He lifted the sheet off of Owen's very clean feet. "There was no blood at the scene—that was my first clue—but I wanted to run the autopsy test before I planted anything in your head. Sometimes I'm wrong, but rarely." He grinned. "This is definitely barbwire electric fencing. See." He grabbed a piece off the tray and wrapped it around Owen's ankles. The holes matched perfectly. "Check this out."

I followed him over to the sink, where he'd taken out the organs for examination and weighed them. He held Owen's heart in his hands.

"This is damage to the heart caused by the electric shock." He pointed and I leaned over to get a better look. "Whoever did this poisoned him through his drink. It was likely antifreeze, so Owen didn't taste it." He put the heart down and picked up the vial of blood. "Very small traces. They gave him just enough to kill him. They knew what they were doing. Then once he was dead, they really wanted to make sure he wasn't coming back by giving him a good jolt of electricity."

Poppa stood over near the report. "What about his feet?"

"What do you think about him having no shoes? Was he placed at the scene?" I asked.

"Definitely." Max nodded his head. "I think he went to see someone he's friends with or thought he was friends with. Took his shoes off at the door and wherever that was is where he was murdered," Max said. Poppa's analysis sounded pretty spot on. Max continued, "Everything else on the autopsy is normal but the damage of the heart. Ears, nose, eyes all symmetrical, body fluids functioning."

Poppa read the autopsy where I skimmed down to the nitty gritty.

"The facts are these." I was looking at Max, but talking to Poppa. "Owen Godbey was murdered. His initial cause of death is poison from a drink and a little oomph with the electric shock for good measure. Then there's Myrna, who had fired Owen."

"She what?" Max's jaw dropped. "When did this happen? And why on Earth didn't she say anything last night?"

"According to her, she fired him a couple of days ago because she caught him with his hands in her recipe box she keeps in the greenhouse. A recipe box that was made by her aunt to help grow the best flowers around. And she didn't tell us because she wanted to call in Wally Lamb because she knew it looked bad."

"This case is getting stranger and stranger." Max peeled off his gloves and rested his behind on the edge of the counter. "So you are thinking Myrna?"

"Not necessarily. First off, if it was Myrna, she had to have help, because she is no bigger than a minute and there is no way on this earth that she carried him to the greenhouse and plunked him down inside. Besides," I reminded him, "she's worked too hard on those tomatoes to even think about not moving them first."

"We can't say she did it in haste because poisoning and the

electric fence were definitely premediated." Max's voice fell away. Both of us were stumped.

"I don't know anyone who didn't like Owen." Max scratched his chin. "Except Sandy Godbey. Have you checked her out?"

"Betty Murphy is doing it as we speak." I looked down at my walkie-talkie. It was unusual not to have heard from Betty and that worried me. Betty might be older and hard of hearing, but she could find things better than my old hound dog. She had all her fingers in different little gossip circles.

"If anyone can find Sandy, it's Betty." Max grinned. "Or Edna Easterly."

"Yep. You're right." I winked. "Edna Easterly has been trying to steal her from me for years for the *Chronicle*'s gossip column. Both of those women might have a tidbit of information here and there that I can piece together."

Poppa smiled. "You sure are smart, Kenni-bug. Edna knows everything that goes on around here, including the likes of Sandy Godbey."

"There is a little snafu with this mess." Max's words hung between us as I waited to hear the rest. "Owen and his ex-wife Sandy had made arrangements and he never changed them."

"I'm assuming since you are getting him ready for cremation that was in there." My brows furrowed because this wasn't news.

"Yes, he is to be cremated, but his remains are to go to Sandy." He eased himself up from the counter and solidly stood on his two feet. "Which means by law I can't give him over to Stanley as he is insisting."

"Then this is more reason for me to find Sandy." I sure hoped Betty Murphy was able to use her gossip resources to find her. Or that Edna would.

"That's not all." The tone of his voice made me pause. "He wants to be cremated with his truck."

"His truck?" I questioned whether I heard him correctly.

"He did love that old truck." Max shrugged. "And I've cremated beloved pets for some and kept them here or even had the deceased's family members bring in the remains so they could be cremated again or stuck in the casket."

"But a hunk of junk?" My instincts told me something wasn't right here.

Poppa ghosted next to me. "Something tells me to get to that truck."

"I agree," I said, my voice lowered.

"You agree to what?" Max asked, handing me a piece of paper.

"Um..." I bit my lip. "I agree you can't give Owen's remains to Stanley. It's against the law."

I looked down at the paper. It was a copy of the arrangements Owen and Sandy had made. It specifically said that Owen was to be cremated along with his truck. There was an impound lot over in Clay's Ferry, a town next to ours that was still considered small but bigger than Cottonwood.

"Calling all units, calling all units." Betty's shrill voice cracked over the walkie-talkie.

"Go ahead." Finn's voice came across, catching me a little off guard. Up until now, all units had been just me.

"I'm here," I said back, my ear tilted.

"I didn't hear anything about Sandy Godbey yet, but I've got feelers out. But I did get some information that is new to me." She clicked off.

"What is that?" I asked.

"Did you know that after Myrna fired Owen, he went to work for Rowdy Hart? I even heard they were pretty good friends. He might know something." Betty's voice cracked. "I'll check on it and let you know if I hear anything."

"Kenni, I just left Tractor Supply, where I got invited to

Cole's tonight." Finn had found his in. "As for the electric fence, they haven't sold that type of fencing in years."

"Thanks, Finn and Betty. I'm going to go follow up on a lead and I'll meet you back at the office later." I clicked off and looked at Max. "When are you going to tell Stanley he can't have the remains?"

"Sign off on the autopsy, I'll give you a copy, and then I'll cremate him." Max's face grew still. "Then I'll call Stanley and tell him. He is not going to be happy."

"Let me look at the truck before you have it hauled off to the impound lot." I walked over to the counter and signed the autopsy paper.

"Too late." Max's lips turned down. "I already called them to pick it up."

"Crap." I grabbed my copy of the autopsy and ran out of the morgue.

Chapter Eleven

I jumped in the Jeep and grabbed the old siren beacon from the backseat. After I rolled down the window and licked the suction cup, I stuck it on top of the roof and flipped the switch. The old siren blared and everyone pulled out of the way when they saw me coming.

"That was the best thing I ever bought." The pride showed on Poppa's face. "When Doolittle Bowman and Wyatt Granger wanted me to get those fancy sheriff cars with the built-in lights, I fiddle-faddled them. They always wanted to spend unnecessary funds in the budget."

"I agree." The Wagoneer was pushed to the limits. I had to get to that impound lot before they did anything to Owen's truck. I had to make sure that there wasn't evidence in there.

"Betty," I called in the walkie-talkie.

"Go ahead, Sheriff." I was happy she responded so quickly.

"Finn, are you here?" I asked.

"Over." His voice was solid and straight to the point.

"Betty, I need you to make a copy of the search warrant we'd gotten for Owen Godbey. I forgot my copy on the desk. And then I need you to give that to Finn. This takes precedence over everything."

"Got it," Betty chirped back.

"Finn, I need you to go grab that and bring it to..." I hesitated, looking over at the piece of paper.

"S&S Auto Service," Poppa whispered, reading off the paper.

"S&S Auto Service in Clay's Ferry." I mouthed "thank you" to Poppa and smiled. It was almost like old times. Even though he wasn't supposed to talk to me about open investigations back then, he did. We would cook supper together and talk about his cases, coming up with different scenarios. Some of them were right. Most were not and far-fetched, but it was a lot of fun. That was how I knew I wanted to go into the same line of work.

"Why all of this?" Finn asked.

"Owen and his ex-wife already had funeral arrangements in place. He was to be cremated along with his truck and she is to get the remains. Something tells me that there has to be something in that truck. I at least want to check it out before they smash and burn it."

"I'm out at his trailer now, and there is no truck and no cookbooks either. I'm on my way, Betty. See you shortly, Kenni," Finn's voice echoed out of the walkie-talkie.

"Kenni..." Betty giggled as though she had a secret.

"Sheriff," Finn corrected himself and clicked off.

"Goodbye, Betty." I clicked off.

"You can wipe that grin off your face." I could feel Poppa's stare.

"When you hear his voice, you get a glow that I know all too well."

"I'm just trying to get this murder solved." I kept both hands on the wheel and tried to concentrate on the curvy country road that lead into Clay's Ferry.

"You are just like me in the job department, but just like your mama in the love department." His ghost continued to speak and I tried to tune it out by going faster and faster. "You have the same look on your face she had when she told me about your daddy for the first time."

"Are you back in ghost form to help me solve crimes or talk about nonsense?" My fingers hurt from gripping the wheel.

I had no time for romance. Especially office romances during an election season.

"Poppa?" I looked over and he was gone. I was sure I'd hurt his feelings and wanted to make it right, but he was good at disappearing. Still, I had a job to do and spending time fantasizing about something as silly as a romantic relationship was a waste of time...right now.

S&S Auto was on the outskirts of town and I could see why. Cars upon cars were stacked miles long and the land alone it took for them to have this business was massive.

The chain-link fence was nice and tidy all the way around the perimeter. When I pulled the Jeep inside the gate, I could tell they took their business seriously. The rows of cars were stacked nice and neat, not the typical junk yard or impound lot I'd had to dig through before.

The sign on the front door of the office was turned to open; they closed at five p.m., which was in a few minutes. The bell over the door dinged my arrival and an older woman with her brown hair fixed in a chin-length bob looked up over the computer.

"Hi, there." She had a sweet smile. She stood up. She ran her hand down her peach knit top and stopped just shy of the waist of her brown trousers. "What can I help you with today, Sheriff?" she asked.

"I'm Sheriff Lowry from Cottonwood." I stepped up to the desk and handed her one of my business cards from the front pocket of my shirt. "I'm here to inquire about a truck that belong to Owen Godbey."

"Let me see." She sat back down and ticked away on the

computer. Her eyes drew up to mine. "Yes. The truck was transported earlier this morning."

"I'm assuming in an outfit as big as this, the truck hasn't been destroyed." I prayed it hadn't and there'd been many more vehicles in front of Owen's truck.

"In cases such as this one, we try to get them done as quickly as possible for the family. Closure." She swiveled her eyes upward. The smile she'd worn a few minutes ago was no longer there. Her lips thinned. "Thank you for checking on it." She stood up, her way of politely telling me that my time was up.

"I'm going to ask you if you could pull the truck for me." I might as well start by asking for what I wanted. "I'm going to need to go over the truck before you destroy it."

"I'm sorry, did you say you had a warrant for the truck?" she asked with narrowed eyes.

"Did you know Mr. Godbey?" I asked, since she seemed to be taking this request so personal. "You seem awfully offended by my request."

"I did not, but I do take our clients personally and when you come in here asking for me to bring the truck back out, I'm assuming it's for police business and for that I'd need a warrant, not a nice smile and worn-out looking business card." The bitter words spilled out of her mouth.

"Hey." Finn bolted through the door. His chest heaved up and down. "I hurried to get this here." He handed me the warrant issued by the judge and bent over to catch his breath.

"I do have a warrant." I handed it to the woman.

She took it and looked it over before she got on the phone. She turned her back to us and whispered to the other person on the line.

"It will be up in a moment. Did you bring a tow?" she asked.

"I can drive it back to Cottonwood." I said and walked outside, Finn following. When we were safely out of earshot, I said, "She was all smiles and pretty ponies when I walked in there. When I asked about the truck, she got a couple cups of nuts asking for the warrant. I'm going to need you to bring me back to grab my Jeep later," I said. Finn was a good deputy so far.

I opened the door of the Wagoneer and took out a couple of pairs of gloves.

"Will do," he said. The rattle of metal sounded in the background. "I hope this truck has some evidence or answers because nothing substantial is really turning up so far."

He was right. The only thing we had was pure speculation.

The truck came barreling down one of the car aisles. A big burly man with a curly mullet got out. He wore a pair of blue mechanic overalls.

"You sure are lucky you made it here in time." He patted the truck. "This baby was next."

"We can take it from here." I stepped up and took Owen's keys from him. "Thank you."

I put on the gloves and opened the door. I noticed the seats had been slashed up. "What happened to the seats?" I called after the man.

"Beats me." He lifted his hands in the air. "It was that way when I picked it up."

"It wasn't that way when I put the police tape around it last night," I said.

"Listen, lady." He looked at me and I tapped my five-point sheriff's star. "Sheriff. I only do what I'm told. I got the order this morning when I got here and drove over to Cottonwood, put the thing on my tow, and brought it here."

"What did you do with the police tape?" I questioned.

"There was no police tape on the truck or I would've called to our dispatch." He seemed like a man who followed protocol. For some reason I believed him. "They said the keys were in the floorboard. So I put them in the ignition to loosen the wheels and off I went. I noticed how messed up the seats were, but didn't think nothing of it. We usually don't get calls to come pick up Mercedes to bring and destroy, so it's typical to what I usually see. Junk."

Without another word, I got in the truck and pulled out of the impound lot, but not without looking back in the rearview mirror, where I could see the woman from the office staring at me as I drove off.

For an old truck, it really did have great pick up and the engine was smooth. Owen did take care of it, but someone wanted to get ahold of it, and for what? I slid my hands in and out of the rips as I drove, just to see if I found anything. By the looks of it, the person who ripped up the seats would stop at nothing to find exactly what they were looking for and apparently what Owen had, they wanted.

It wasn't until I parked in the alley behind Cowboy's Catfish that I really got a good gander at the truck.

Finn pulled up and parked behind me.

"This thing is a mess." Betty looked inside, her pocketbook hooked in the crook of her arm. It was quittin' time and she wasn't about to stay another minute longer. "I've switched over dispatch and am heading over to craft night at Lulu's. Duke's inside." It wasn't unusual for the small towns in Kentucky to combine their dispatch services after hours.

"What is the craft this week?" I asked, knowing Lulu always did something different and it was a big time for the women.

"Stained glass." She drew her shoulders up and together. "I've always wanted to try."

"That sounds like fun." I smiled at her. I loved that at her age she still wanted to have a job and go out within the community. Most of her friends were in the retirement community and happy to be there.

"It's also interesting that the piece of glass you had for evidence was stained glass." Betty turned and walked down the alley.

"What?" I asked.

"Some of the evidence came back from the lab. On the fax machine." She walked on off.

Finn and I rushed into the office.

"The report says that the glass was stained-glass fragments and there were some specks of dirt that turned out to be hog feces." Finn read the paper. It was our first real clue.

"Pig poop?" My nose curled. "That could explain where the barbwire had come from. I know hog farmers use electric fence to keep the coyotes out. And the only family I know in town that raise hogs are the Harts."

"As in Katy Lee?" Finn asked about one of my best friends.

"As in Rowdy Hart, Katy's brother." I sucked in a deep breath. "In fact, Betty told me that he'd heard Owen had been working for Rowdy over at the cemetery since Myrna fired him."

"But how well do you know Rowdy?" Finn asked. "He's a big dude. He could definitely pick up Owen. I won't go to Cole's. I'll head on over to Rowdy's with you."

"No, I want you to go to Cole's because Rowdy goes there too." It would be interesting to see how Rowdy acted around Finn. "He can put away a few cold ones and maybe it'll loosen up his lips, if you know what I mean."

"I do." He grinned. "If you need me, I'm here."

"Let me take a quick look at the truck before you drive me back to my Jeep."

We walked back outside and after we put gloves on, Finn went to the driver's side and I went to the passenger side.

It looked like the contents of the glovebox had been rummaged through and thrown on the floorboard. The truck's registration, insurance card from Rowdy's family insurance company, and a composition notebook were among the items. I thumbed through the notebook. Page after page, there were recipes written down in frilly handwriting. I flipped it over to the front page—in faded ink it read "Property of Rae Lynn Godbey."

"Finn," I gasped. "I think we just got what everyone seems to be looking for."

"You found the cookbook?" he asked and looked up. Our eyes met. Suddenly all of my common sense skittered and I felt all giddy.

I couldn't tell if my heart was racing because I could feel his breath on my face, or that I had just found the infamous cookbook, or that the touch of his fingers ran up through my arms after I handed it to him.

"I, um..." I closed my eyes and got my composure. "And we were looking for a hardback cookbook."

I turned around and smiled so he didn't see.

Chapter Twelve

As Finn drove me back to Clay's Ferry, poor Duke was stuffed in the backseat of Finn's Dodge Charger. His tongue was sticking out and he was panting. His breath was so bad, I would've rather he farted.

Finn tried to be polite and rolled down his window, which only made Duke crazier as he lunged his body over to Finn's side and stuck his head out the window.

As Finn wrestled with Duke, I quickly thumbed through the pages of the cookbook. There wasn't anything special that stuck out to me, but I was far from a chef. I was able to cook the basics and stick things in the Crock-Pot, but beyond that it was dining out. There was an okra recipe, but nothing I saw in it stood out, except that she used buttermilk to coat them along with cornmeal. She used a cast-iron skillet to fry, which seemed a little messy to me, but maybe that was her secret since I'd only known it fried in a fryer. I thought that I might try my hand out in the kitchen and make it just to see what all the fuss was about.

Maybe it was just the fact that Rae Lynn was a good cook and she had that special touch for this particular recipe; she just might've added a dash here or there like most southern women did. Who knew? Somehow this book had something to do with Owen. But what?

"I'll call you when I get out of Cole's," Finn said when he parked at the impound.

There was something about him and his confidence that inspired me. I wanted to do my best and I cared what he thought about me.

"I'm going to go try my hand at stained glass," I informed him and stared into his brown eyes. There was a warm glow filling my chest. I gulped. "I'll let you know who's there and if I find out anything. I don't think it's a coincidence that someone knifed his truck."

"Sounds good." Finn's smile broadened. "But you'll need to get out of the car so we can do that."

"Sheriff," he called after me before I shut the door. His smile faded a little when I looked back at him. "We will figure this out. I know that you don't like people looking out for you, but you be careful."

"I'm fine." I waved him off and grabbed my bag. I stood there and watched while he zoomed off as Duke relieved himself before our ride back to Cottonwood.

I'm fine since it's you that's looking out after me. I bit my lip at how strangely flattered I was by his interest, but I knew there was nothing I could do about it. We were coworkers. It wouldn't look good, especially getting close to election season. I gripped the handle of the bag and put all my energy into it before I opened the driver's door to let Duke jump in.

"Go on." I encouraged him to move to his spot on the passenger seat.

He looked back at me. "What?" I asked and glanced around him.

My eyes narrowed on a knife stabbed in the passenger seat of my truck. Attached to the blade was a blank dog tag in the shape of a bone.

"Duke." I patted him out of the Jeep and opened the back

door for him to sit in the backseat. I wasn't about to touch the knife.

Fiery anger swelled up in me. Someone was sending me a message, and I didn't take threats too kindly. I glanced up at the office of S&S—it was dark. I looked up at the roofline of the office and dragged my eyes down the gutter. I counted two different video cameras.

I put my bag on the front seat and took out my camera. I snapped all sorts of photos of the knife from different angles and close-ups. I took photos of the office, the space between my Jeep and the office, the road around my Jeep, and made a note to come back for the security footage.

After I snapped gloves on my hands, I took the knife out and brought it up to my face. The shell handle was plastic and the knife was dull. It reminded me of a knife my Poppa would've given me as a child. I put the knife and the tag in an evidence bag.

It wasn't a knife that could do any real damage, but it was there to send a message. Someone didn't like me snooping around. Duke jumped up to the passenger seat next to me and poked his nose on the window.

"Too bad." I leaned over and rolled down the window. Duke draped his front paws on the window ledge. I threw it in gear and headed straight to Cottonwood, namely Lulu's Boutique. I used one hand to steer and the other to rub down Duke's back. I could deal with someone threatening me. But messing with my dog was a whole other ballgame.

"I'll protect you." I looked over at Duke. His tongue was flapping out of his mouth, his ears pushed back as he let the wind blow around him as we zoomed back into town.

I kept an extra change of clothes in my car for times like these. Though I was always on duty, when I did something that I considered after hours, I made sure to change into my street clothes. Even though I'd known these women all my life, there was something about the uniform that made them more standoffish.

I grabbed my bag and the clothes and held the door open for Duke to join me. There was a light coming from the craft room and the sounds of laughter spilled out into the night. Duke made our presence known before I did.

"Hi, Duke!" The greetings were echoed and overlapping each other from different women.

"Are you by yourself?" Lulu asked him in a soft baby voice.

It wasn't unusual for Duke to wander around Cottonwood. Everyone knew him and they would drop him off on Free Row or give dispatch a call if he was out too long to make sure I knew where he was.

"I hope I get a warm welcome like Duke." The room was filled with most of my mama's friends, including her. I couldn't help but wonder if any of them had anything to do with Owen. Any of them might say they'd kill to get a look at the cookbook but probably wouldn't actually do it. Or would they? I gripped the handles of my bag a little tighter.

"You sure do, Kendrick." Lulu smiled. Her black razor-cut short hair was a little spikier on the top this evening. She had on a chunky glass necklace and glass-bead bracelets going up her arm. She was always very stylish and tonight was no different. "We are so excited to see you. Don't you love the pansy stained-glass stepping stone we are going to make?" She patted the round cement stone with three green stained-glass stems with purple pansy petals. It was really pretty. "It will take a couple of classes."

"Yoo-hoo!" Mama spotted me first thing. She shooed a hand at Viola White, who was sitting next to her. "Move on down so Kenni can sit here."

Viola grumbled under her breath.

"It's okay, Viola." I pointed to an open chair next to Edna Easterly. "I'm gonna sit right here in case I need to go."

Mama glared. She gritted her teeth under a fake smile. "I don't give a hoot or a holler if you get called out or not. You will come sit right here by your mama." She patted the seat next to her.

"You might as well." Viola's lips pinched. "I've already moved."

Edna and I exchanged glances. She pulled a piece of paper out of her notebook, the one she never left home without—she scribbled God-knows-what in the thing. She slid the paper across the craft table when I walked by. I stopped and bent down with my palm over the paper.

"Good evening, Edna." I smiled.

"You got the killer yet?" Edna asked, keeping up with the pain-in-the-neck banter she always gave me when we ran into each other.

"You know I can't reveal anything." I winked and played along, knowing if she and I didn't have these types of exchanges when were seen together, everyone in town would know something was up.

"So that means that you have no leads in Owen Godbey's murder?" she asked.

"Murder?" A few gasps blanketed the room. As if they hadn't already heard.

I glared at Betty. Her gasp was the loudest.

I pulled myself up to a straight standing position and put the paper in my bag.

"Hi." I stopped by the table where my friend Katy Lee Hart was sitting. "What's going on?"

"Nothing. I hear you are super busy." She smiled. "We were thinking about getting together tomorrow night for a movie night." She referred to our group of friends.

"Can't. I have a town-council meeting. You aren't coming?" I laughed inwardly, recalling the last one we had, when I fell off the stage and landed in Finn's strong arms. My heart fluttered thinking about it. I hadn't forgotten about those arms since. "I'm going to propose a site for a sheriff's office."

"I might come just for the fireworks," she said, knowing I was going to have a hard time passing my ideas on to the town council. "How's the case going?"

"I do have a question for you about electric fencing." It was the perfect opportunity to ask her. "I know Rowdy has some hogs. Does he use high-grade electric fencing?"

"Oh no." She shook her head. "He never has. He thinks it's inhumane. He hated it when Daddy used it, so when he took over the hogs and moved them to his place, he did away with it."

"Darn." I pretended to be sad. "I had a couple of questions about it. But I did find out that he was so nice to Owen by giving him some odd jobs at the cemetery."

"If you want to call it that." She rolled her eyes. "I wouldn't call smoking pot a job."

"Huh?" That was the last thing I thought I'd hear.

"Yeah. I went out to the farm to give Owen his new home insurance policy and get a signature and they were smoking pot on the back porch. Rowdy tried to cover it up, but I know the smell of pot. Plus, Owen's eyes were all glazed over and he was laughing about nothing," she said. "Then the next thing I know, Owen is dead."

"When was this?" I asked.

"The day Owen died. Or was murdered," she corrected herself.

"Ladies, tonight we leave work on the outside." Lulu walked over and interrupted our little powwow. I was glad that she did because Katy Lee had thrown me for a loop. Now I knew where Owen had been on the day of his death.

"There is no negative energy in the creative craft room," Lulu chirped.

"There is the linger of an On The Run hotdog," Inez Godbey blurted out from the corner of the room where she sat all alone. Our eyes met. She looked away. Her fingers fiddled with the small plastic cups filled with colorful glass that were on the table in front of her.

Lulu didn't like the fact someone smelled something other than the candles she sold up front in the boutique. She quickly ran around the room spraying some aerosol cans in the air and fanning the odor with her hand.

"Stop that," Myrna Savage spat when she walked in the craft room with a tomato plant nestled in her arms. She shielded the plant with her hand. "Don't you dare get those chemicals around my plant."

"Sorry, Myrna." Lulu quickly changed directions.

I went to the bathroom to change my clothes and no sooner than I walked out the bathroom door did I hear a full-on cat fight between Myrna Savage and Inez Godbey.

"I dare you to sit next to me after what you've done to our family." Inez stood up and planted her palms on the craft table. She glared at Myrna.

"Why are you hollerin' like a stuck pig?" Myrna put her plant down on the table.

"You gonna sit over there all high and mighty like you didn't kill Owen? I'd be ashamed if I were you," Inez said as tears rolled down her face.

As profanities flew out of their mouths, everyone else's mouths dropped and eyes nearly popped right out of their sockets.

"I knew I shouldn't have come here." Inez grabbed her bag; her chair fell over and thumped on the floor. "But no." Her head swayed side to side. "Stanley told me to go, get out of the house, it's good for your soul. Do something creative." She flung her purse in the air, tossing it over her shoulder, and knocked the tomato plant in the process.

The plant catapulted into the air and hit the wall with a thud. The soil and small tomato seeds dripped down the wall. It was a scene just like the greenhouse.

"All hell's about to break loose." Edna pushed me out of the way, her camera snapping as the two women continued to fight.

"You low-down dirty..." Myrna said some words not fittin' to hear before she scurried toward Inez, but not before I got in between them.

"Ladies." I stepped in and dropped my bag on the floor. My uniform tumbled out. I left it there for the time being so I could calm the two of them down. "There is no need to act like this."

"Kenni, did you see what she did to my prize tomato?" Myrna pointed a finger at Inez.

"Pointing is not polite," Mama chimed in. We all turned and stared at her. I put my hand up like a stop sign.

"That's two people in her family that have sabotaged me. First, Owen." Myrna spat his name as if there was a bitter taste in her mouth. "Now you." She jutted the finger a little more forward.

"I dare you to say another word about Owen." Inez looked at me. "Well, here she is, Sheriff. Do your job. Arrest her."

"Arrest me?" Myrna drew back. "For what? I think you should be arrested for sabotaging my tomatoes." Myrna pointed back. "I want to make a citizen's arrest."

"Can you stop taking pictures?" I asked Edna, who was standing completely on top of the craft table trying to take photos from all angles.

Lulu slid her body down the wall, giving up on trying to create peace. She cried in the palms of her hands. Chaos was in full swing.

Edna pulled the camera from her face. She said, "Nope. Lead story tomorrow." She disappeared back behind the lens.

"I am not going to arrest anyone for anything." I made them stay a good distance apart. "Now, let's go back to our seats so we can enjoy a night with friends."

"I'll do no such thing." Myrna planted her hands on her hips. "If she's staying, I'm leaving."

"You can't leave," Lulu sobbed. "You're teaching the class."

"Don't you worry. I'm out of here." Inez jerked around. "But I don't have a ride. Stanley brought me."

"I'll take you home." I was going to stop by her house anyway with the Derby Pie Finn had offered, which was upstairs in his apartment. "I'll come to craft night another time. Duke." I snapped my fingers and he came to attention.

"Are you sure?" she asked.

"I am." I smiled and waited for her to go outside. I bid goodnight to everyone, but not without making a mental note that of all people, Myrna Savage was teaching the class. We'd found the broken stained glass at the scene. Though it wasn't a direct link to Owen's murder, it still tugged at my gut.

"Can you wait right here with Duke for a minute? I need to tell Finn something." I gestured to the stairs leading up to the apartment, knowing Finn wasn't in there, but the Derby Pie was.

Inez simply nodded.

With my bump key, I jimmied the lock and let myself in. The phone was ringing when I helped myself to his freezer and pulled out the pie. I was sure he wouldn't mind.

The answering machine picked up and a sultry female voice came over the speaker.

"Hey, handsome," the woman said. "I'm excited about this weekend. I really can't believe you called. I re-e-e-ally can't believe that you are living in some podunk town and left me all alone." I didn't like how she sounded. "But you have all weekend to make up for that. I can't wait to see you talk with all those crazy sayings you're learning. What was the pig and lipstick one again?" She laughed. Images of her, or how I pictured her, flowed through my head. "Call me before you come. Finley," she called him by his full name, "remember that I love you. Always."

She hung up.

My jaw dropped. I was sick to my stomach thinking about what was going on this weekend with the sultry-voiced woman. The pie was calling me to eat it. But I couldn't. I had promised to do some investigative work with it by giving it to Inez.

"He's a coworker," I reminded myself, but the memory of how he looked at me on the Ferris wheel a couple of nights ago made me feel like we were more. At least I'd thought so. Or maybe it was my own crazy mind wishing it was more. "He's just a coworker. Poppa was right." I swallowed hard.

I walked over to the counter where the answering machine was sitting and eyed the blinking red button. I put my finger on the erase button. I bit my lip. I shook my head and pulled my hand away. I took a step back and stepped on one of Finn's stray shoes and teetered, grabbing the counter, accidentally side-swiping the answering machine.

"Messages erased," the mechanical voice said over the speaker.

"No. No." I frantically pushed the play button, totally regretting what I had just done.

"No messages," the mechanical voice teased me.

"Oh God." I groaned and looked at the pie in my hand. "Inez."

I had completely forgotten about Inez waiting for me. I had lost it. It was a fact. I rushed out of the apartment.

"Are you okay?" Inez asked. She was sitting on the bottom step petting Duke. He was staring at her eyes. His ears drew back as she ran her long nails down the crown of his head.

"I'm fine." I held up the pie. "I'd gotten this pie earlier for you. I was going to stop by your house with it after the craft class."

My heart was racing. I still couldn't believe I'd just erased Finn's message. What was wrong with me?

"That's awful kind of you." She smiled and stood up. "Lulu brought your bag out."

"I totally forgot it back there." I handed her the pie in exchange for the bag. I took a quick peek inside and pushed my uniform to the side. The composition book was still there. I got my keys out from the bottom of the bag. "You ready?"

"I am." She and I walked to the Jeep.

Duke automatically jumped in the back like he did when I had someone up front. Inez helped herself to the passenger side and placed the pie next to us on the center console.

"How is Stanley holding up?" I started in with the basic question. "I couldn't imagine."

"Are you asking as a friend or sheriff?" She hooked her seatbelt in and stared ahead with her hands in her lap.

"As a concerned friend." I started the Jeep up and pulled out.

"He's devastated." Her voice cracked. "He's so strong and refuses to give into his feelings. I told him that it was okay to cry and even bash things in." Her voice trailed off. "I leave him be because he can be so demeaning and cruel when his feelings are hurt or something is on his mind." She stopped as though she were gathering her thoughts. "When he is hurt, angry, or feels like he's been wronged in any way, nothing will stop him from getting what he wants."

"That's a man for you." I gripped the wheel, wondering how I was going to get into how he reacted when I told him.

"You know when Rae Lynn died, it just tore them boys up. Poor Owen went a little off the deep end. He was obsessed with the family cookbook." She shook her head. "Don't get me wrong, Rae Lynn was an excellent cook, but nothing to write home about. She went by the recipes that were passed down by her family. When he got divorced, Sandy knew it would hurt him to ask for the cookbook, so she did."

"She did?" I asked. "What a shame. Get him where it hurts."

My phone chirped a text, but I didn't think it would look good to Inez if the sheriff grabbed her phone and checked out who was texting her while driving. I could hear it now: the sheriff breaks the law. Another rumor that I didn't need to risk starting.

"He's spent the better part of the past year hiding it from her. Stanley told him to hand it over so he can just move on with his life and forget about her, but Owen wouldn't. He wanted to punish Sandy for leaving him." It was like the floodgates had opened. Inez was out of Stanley's reach and she was talking.

She looked out the window and I took the opportunity to slide my phone onto voice record.

"Why on earth wouldn't he just make a copy of the book and give it to her?" I asked.

"Because Rae Lynn said the magic was in the pages. He wanted the original, and now look where it got him." She sobbed. "I don't even think he knew where the damn cookbook was. I bet he lost it."

"I'm so sorry." I turned down Catnip Road. "I am doing all I can to bring his murderer to justice."

"I'm telling you that if you find Sandy Godbey, she'll have the answers. I told Stanley I bet she did Owen in, especially after she lost the last court battle." My ears sprang up. Betty had pulled the court records and there wasn't anything on the docket.

"What happened?" I asked as we turned up the gravel drive.

"They went back to court the morning he died and the judge

sided with Owen. Sandy didn't get her hands on the family cookbook." Inez put her hand on the door handle. "Stanley would die if he knew I was airing out our family laundry to you. But you need to know the facts."

"Then why do you think Myrna had anything to do with it?" I was a little stumped in her thinking.

"I think Myrna helped Sandy. He was found in her greenhouse. She and Sandy were friends, maybe not best friends, but Sandy did help Myrna at Petal Pushers before she moved a couple of months ago and that's when Owen started to help. Picked up where Sandy left off." She uncovered another thing Myrna had covered up. "It just isn't a coincidence to me." She shrugged before she got out. "That's all."

Myrna might not have been able to put Owen in the greenhouse, but Myrna and Sandy together could've. The more and more I heard about Owen's relationships, the more Myrna looked guilty.

The front porch light switched on. The door opened. Stanley Godbey stood as big as life in the door frame, Poppa standing behind him with his fingers held up in the okay sign.

"I didn't know he was home. I've got to go." The look of fear set in her eyes and she slammed the door without looking back.

"But your pie," I grumbled from the inside the Jeep as the front porch light flipped off, telling me I was not welcome there.

There was something going on behind that door. Inez was scared of Stanley. Stanley might not have wanted her to talk to the sheriff, but that was not the fear I'd seen on her face as she scrambled to get out of the Jeep.

Poppa appeared next to me in the passenger seat. "That was interesting."

"Yeah. Bone chilling." I recalled Stanley's eyes.

"He definitely doesn't like anyone to know their business," Poppa said. "He asked Inez what she'd said to you and she said nothing about them, but you talked about Owen and Sandy. He told her to keep her mouth shut about the family business. The issues between him and Owen were now water under the bridge."

My mind was reeling with all sorts of possible situations. Talking them out with Poppa always gave me some clarity.

The gravel spit up under the tires. "If there was a family rift like Ruby said, then Stanley could be a suspect. But why? Why would he want to murder his own brother?" I paused. "Then there's Myrna. She definitely has a motive. If he was trying to steal her cherished recipe to help grow the vegetables, she could've done it out of anger. Or she was a good friend to Sandy Godbey, who I have to find because she's definitely a suspect."

"You have at least three people who you need to investigate." Poppa broke down the big picture, which was something I was learning to do. Not that I didn't know how to be a sheriff. I did. It was all this murder stuff that was new to me. "Myrna and Sandy are tied."

"Which means I need to find Sandy to help rule her out and find out about Myrna's friendship with her. And we still can't leave Myrna out because she really doesn't have an alibi." In no time Poppa, Duke, and I were back on Free Row and had pulled into the driveway.

"Sometimes a good night's sleep will help your mind relax and give you a fresh look on things in the morning." Poppa ghosted out of the Jeep.

I grabbed my bag from the floorboard and the pie. Duke jumped out after me and sprinted toward the back of the house, followed up by a deep barking.

The rustle of footsteps and the jingle of a fence caught my attention. I sat my bag and pie on the ground. I unzipped my bag and pulled out my Colt .45.

"Hold it right there!" I screamed with my elbows slightly

cocked, arms extended, and gun pointing into the dark. "Sheriff!"

Duke continued to go nuts, running up and down the fence line. I kicked the gate, busting it open, and ran to the back of my yard, where I heard someone running across my neighbor's pavement.

"Next time I'll shoot!" I yelled, deciding not to give chase. For one, I didn't have backup and two, they ran off.

My nostrils flared as I tried to suck deep breaths in and out, releasing the adrenaline that'd found a nice fearful place deep in my bones.

I wanted to say it was just a coincidence from living on Free Row, but when I walked into the house and saw that it looked like a tornado had ripped through it, I knew it was personal.

The only thing I could do right then was eat the pie. I did.

Chapter Thirteen

"Why didn't you call me?" Finn asked when we met up for breakfast at Ben's. The morning sunshine flooded the restaurant window and broke on his face. His brown eyes twinkled with concern.

"You were busy at Cole's and I filled out my own report, photos and all. I've already uploaded it." I leaned back in the chair across from him and let Ben Harrison fill up the two empty cups of coffee in front of me. One for me, and another for me.

"Would you like a coffee?" Ben asked Finn.

"Please." Finn pushed his empty cup toward the edge of the table.

As he filled up the cup, Ben rattled off the specials. He glanced at me. "The usual?"

"Yes. But I'm going to need extra syrup and powdered sugar today." The jolt of sugar was exactly what I needed to wake me up this morning. Granted, I might crash in a couple of hours.

"You?" Ben pointed the pen at Finn.

"I'll have what she's having." Finn closed the menu and put it back between the salt and pepper shakers.

I wasn't going to lie to myself. It didn't feel good that someone had broken into my house. There was no way I was going to let Finn know that it had scared the bejesus out of me and I'd had a tight grip on Duke all night, not to mention my pistol.

"I told you I was going to stay up all night and watch out." Poppa grumbled next to me, his nose stuck in my coffee cup. "I sure do wish I could have a big sip of that."

I smiled.

"What?" Finn's brows formed a V. "What's the big smile for?"

"I have Sandy Godbey's address." Of course, I was smiling at Poppa; I just made a good cover up. I picked my bag up off the ground.

"How did you get it?" Finn picked up his coffee cup, taking a sip.

"I told Edna I'd give her the exclusive for the paper if she did some digging around for me." I drummed my fingers on the table and looked around.

Inez Godbey, Lulu McClain, and Ruby Smith were seated at the bar. Ruby twirled around on the stool and gave me a little wave with one hand and fiddled with the jade pendent around her neck with the other. She had a matching brooch stuck on her shirt and I wondered if it was an antique find from one of her adventures.

Inez was talking to Edna Easterly. It had to have been an interview, because Edna's head was down and she was writing furiously in that darn notebook.

I stuck my hand in the pants pockets and came up short. I checked all the pockets again before I looked into my bag. The composition book was still in there, but there was no sign of the piece of paper Edna had slipped me at the stained-glass class last night.

"It's not in here." I sat back in the chair with my bag on my lap. My fingers tensed.

"Are you sure you put it in your pants?" Finn asked.

"Positive." I recalled what had happened and told him about the confrontation with Inez and Myrna.

"Myrna was teaching the class?" The information seemed to strike a chord with Finn, just as it had with me.

"Yes. And I'm not sure who picked up my stuff because I had dropped my bag on the floor to stop them from fighting. Everything fell out but the cookbook." I slid my eyes back over to the three women.

They had to be there for the cook-off. Myrna had told me they were on Ben's team. Plus, the three of them were hunched over creating some sort of concoction in clay mixing bowls that had an upside-down picket-fence design around the tops.

Edna lifted her chin in the air, acknowledging me before she sauntered over.

"Sheriff." Her eyes drew down on me.

I used the toe of my boot to push the extra chair at the table out for her to sit.

"I can't find that piece of paper," I whispered to Edna when I leaned forward and picked up the coffee cup. "I have no idea where it went. I put it in my pants pocket before I changed and now it's gone." I took a sip and held the cup in my fingertips in front of my face.

"Can you recall your steps?" Finn raked his brown hair with his fingers. His dark eyes had a reserve I couldn't put my finger on.

"I went to your apartment." I stopped myself from talking when I remembered I'd erased his message on his answering machine. "To get the pie," I finally finished.

"You threw your bag on the floor and I think Myrna picked it up." Edna's eyes narrowed as if she were trying to remember. "Some of your stuff fell out. Are you sure you put the paper in your pocket?"

"I was so focused on making sure people didn't think you

and I were playing too nice, so I'm not sure of anything." The only thing I did remember for sure was erasing Finn's message.

"After Myrna picked up your stuff, Lulu took the bag outside." Edna shrugged.

"And that is how Inez got it." I snapped my fingers and leaned back in the chair, finishing off the last sips of my first cup.

"Is this on or off the record?" Edna asked. She was an ever-changing mystery to me. One minute she wanted everything on the record and off the next.

"It's off for right now, but when you get the exclusive, you can put it in there because someone took the paper." I wasn't sure if I was trying to convince myself that someone took it or if I was trying not to look inadequate in front of Finn.

If Myrna knew I was watching her, she'd be watching my every move and would have seen Edna slip me a piece of paper. Out of curiosity, she used the opportunity to grab my things and slip the paper out of my pants pocket. "Can I get the address again?"

"Here it is." Edna flipped through her notepad. "Take a picture of it with your phone."

"I'll do better than that." I took my phone out. "I'll put the address in my maps right now because I'm going to see Sandy first thing."

"Not without me." Finn pulled his forearms off the edge of the table, allowing room for Ben to put the food down in front of him. Finn looked at the plate.

"You have a problem with your food?" Ben asked.

"Pancakes with eggs on top with syrup and powdered sugar." Finn shook his head. "I shouldn't be surprised, but I am."

"It's her favorite." Ben glanced at me and smiled. "I know that look."

"What look?" Finn asked.

"She's ready to go. I'll get you a coffee to go and a to-go box." Ben turned around.

"Is he right?" Finn cut into the short stack with his fork and stuck it in his mouth.

"He is." I looked over the table at Finn. Boy, was I wrong. He was no more interested in me than he was in Ruby Smith at the counter stirring her little heart out. Ben Harrison could read me like a book, but my partner had no idea who I was outside of this uniform.

Yet again, Poppa was right.

"Let me know what else I can do." Edna got up from the table and excused herself just as Ben came back with the to-go cups and containers. "Don't forget," she reminded me. "Exclusive."

"I'll ride along with you and tell you about last night at Cole's." Finn took a few more quick bites of his breakfast while I scooped mine into a box. "That was an eye-opener." There was a sharp edge to his laugh. "I spent a lot of time undercover with the mob in Chicago before the reserves and they were nothing like these good ole boys with their gambling and booze."

"Yes, they do take their booze seriously." A melancholic frown flitted across my face. "My Poppa always said that if that was the worst thing that went on around here, Cottonwood was going to be A-OK."

"Your Poppa was a smart man. I'm sorry I didn't get to meet him." Finn reached over and patted my hand.

"I bet you are." Poppa shook a fist at Finn. "I'd run you right out of town." Poppa bounced on the tips of his toes like he was going to do some boxing.

"Who was there?" I had to start talking and ignore Poppa to keep from busting out laughing. I dragged my hand out from underneath Finn's.

"All the major players." Finn grabbed my bag off the floor for me. "Mayor Ryland, Luke Jones, Stanley Godbey, Rowdy Hart."

"Are you going to eat your eggs?" I asked.

"No." He shook his head and I scraped them off the top of his pancakes and into a container.

We threw down a few bucks to cover the bill and headed out the door to the Wagoneer. Duke's paws were draped over the passenger window, his head rested on the window ledge and his eyes closed. His nose shifted side to side, his eyes popped open, and he darted to sitting when he saw the box in my hand. Poppa was nowhere around.

"Here, buddy." I opened the back door of the Jeep and he hopped from the front seat to the back. I opened the container with Finn's eggs, letting Duke eat them.

"There was a lot of talk about Owen and why someone wanted to kill him." Finn stared straight ahead on our way out of town.

"How did Stanley act?" I asked.

"He was quiet. He had a few beers and then went home after they started talking about Owen's finances." Finn tapped his finger on the window. "It got me thinking."

"About?" I asked.

"What if he owed someone money? They said he was low on funds since Sandy had taken him back to court and he didn't have money to pay for an attorney. They also said he stopped taking his medicine for his arthritis because of the cost. Then there was Rowdy Hart." His voice trailed off.

"What about him?" I asked. "Because I did find out that he doesn't use electric fence, but he and Owen were at his house smoking pot the day Owen was murdered."

"Max hadn't gotten back to you about anything in Owen's system?" Finn's voice was resigned.

"No, only that he suspects antifreeze was the poison. You know those reports can take days, even weeks." I sighed and pulled onto what was Sandy's street, according to my maps. "I want to stop by and question Rowdy. He might know someone who does use that fencing, plus he might've been the last person to see Owen alive."

"He might be able to tell us where Owen went after he left Rowdy's," Finn noted. "After I left Cole's, I went back to the office and put together a few timelines on that dry-erase board you never use. I'm a visual person, so I need to write down all the facts we have. Sometimes it helps me put together the pieces and see where there are holes. It's like a spider grid. Everyone is connected somehow and it will help us make connections easier."

"Great idea." I didn't want to tell him that was what I did with Poppa when he was alive and now that he was in ghost form we did it verbally. "It will definitely help. I look forward to seeing it."

I kept the conversation very professional; I needed to since I'd heard the woman on his voicemail.

"According to my maps app, Sandy lives in Clay's Ferry. Which makes it perfect for me to stop by S&S Auto Salvage to get a look at the video footage from when someone had knifed my seat," I said to Finn.

"Then this should be very interesting." Finn let out a deep sigh.

We pulled up to a newer two-story home. It was half siding and half brick. There were a couple dormer windows. Neat wildflower beds ran across the front of the house in front of the porch with the white fence attached.

"This is it. 510." I pointed to the house number on the plastic mailbox on the left side of the driveway.

As I pulled into the driveway, the garage door was going up.

Finn and I got out. The car was pulling out but stopped when the driver noticed us. The engine died. The door opened and a pair of toned and tanned legs swung out of the car followed by a very young-looking Sandy Godbey.

Her hair looked to be freshly dyed, blond with brown highlights, and cut to her shoulders. It wasn't the frizzy style that I had recalled her having. Her skin was smoother than I remembered, and the lines on the creases of her eyes were gone.

"I wondered how long it would take you to find me." Sandy had on a pair of white shorts, a blue denim shirt, and a pair of neon pink Converse high-tops. A clutch was tucked up under her arm. "Myrna told me you'd been snooping around."

Now I knew Myrna was the one who took the piece of paper from my bag. According to Myrna, she didn't know where Sandy lived. That was stealing and I'd let her know.

"In fact, I was just on my way to come find you." She handed me her cell phone. My dispatch number was on the screen. "I was about to hit dial. Then here you are."

"Why were you coming to see me?" I asked.

"The same reason you're here. About Owen." A couple of her neighbors had gathered on the sidewalk in front of a house. Their heads were together. "Why don't we go inside, Kenni?"

"This is Deputy Finn Vincent." We followed her into the garage. She hit the automatic garage door button to put the door back down. "He's the new deputy we hired since Lonnie retired."

We followed her into the house. The kitchen was the first room. There were white cabinets, gray granite countertops, and gray wood floors.

"Good ole Lonnie. You know..." She placed her purse on the counter, next to an open box of cornmeal. The sunlight flooded through the window. There were two tiny white cat statues sitting on the windowsill. "...Owen really did like him. But I'm sure he would've liked you too, Finn. I mean, Deputy. Move,

Cozmo." She shooed the dark gray-haired cat with light gray stripes that came running from the other room and darted under her feet.

"Thank you. I hate to hear about your loss," Finn started the conversation and snapped his fingers to get the feline's attention.

Cozmo's green eyes stared at Finn's fingers before the cat thought it was a safe finger to get a good scratch from.

"I'm sure you don't, since you're here to see if I killed him." Sandy opened the refrigerator and took out a pitcher of tea. I noticed a carton of buttermilk in the refrigerator before she closed the door. "I just made sun tea and was chilling it in the fridge." She took three glasses out of the cabinet.

I eyed the tea, wondering if she had put antifreeze in it, but when she took a swig of it after she poured herself a glass, I figured I was safe.

"Let's have a seat." She put the pitcher of tea and glasses on a tray and walked over to the white table. "Obviously I didn't kill Owen."

We all took a seat around the table. I put my bag on the floor and took out a pad of paper and pen.

"We didn't say you did. You don't mind if I take a few notes, do you?" I asked.

"I'm fine with that." She crossed her legs.

I wrapped my hand around the glass. The tea was chilled and the perfect orange color like my mama made. "We would like to know the terms of your divorce, as well as the funeral arrangements."

"Oh gosh." She drew her hand to her mouth. Her nails were perfectly manicured and painted pink. "I forgot all about those arrangements." She put on a smile more American than fast food. "What did his brother and Inez say about them?"

"Actually, we didn't tell them anything since his remains do not concern them." I picked up the glass and wet my whistle. "But I'd like to know what you'd like to do about him."

"Follow what we wanted." She shrugged. She was awfully relaxed for the situation. "He wanted to be cremated with that stupid truck. I'll take him to the farm and sprinkle his ashes right in the okra patch."

"To my understanding, he was having a hard time growing okra." I watched her face.

"Myrna said she caught him red-handed in her cigar box." She shook her new hair. "You know Myrna did me a favor by giving him a job when I left him. I knew he was going to need to keep busy."

"What about the okra patch?" Finn moved his head slightly as he looked at her.

"His mama's." Her face went to stone.

"That would be on Stanley and Inez's property." Finn eased back in the chair, crossed his leg, and rested his ankle on the opposite knee. Slowly he tapped the pad of his middle finger on the white table.

Her face remained stern.

"Why did you leave him?" I asked.

"The truth?" she shot back.

"Nothing better," Finn chimed in.

"I was tired of all the bickering between him and Stanley. Inez didn't make it any better. Rae Lynn had really wanted to make a go of the crop. She'd gotten offers from some of those fancy organic stores, but the problem was that Rae Lynn gave Stanley the land with the crop and gave Owen her recipe. She knew they had their differences and that they would have to put them aside in order to work together to get the right soil-to-plant-food ratio that she'd figured out."

"But instead of bringing them together after her death, it divided them even more."

I wrote down everything she'd told me in my notebook.

"Yes. Owen was obsessed with the soil on our property. He wanted Stanley's soil after the will was read." She frowned at the memory. "He spent every single dollar we had buying products to make the soil like Stanley's. He even snuck over to Stanley's and took a sample of the soil. God knows how much he spent. That was the last bit of money we had saved for his medicine and the last straw. So I left. When Myrna told me about him trying to steal from her, I knew it was all she wrote."

"All she wrote?" An odd mingling of wariness and amusement was in Finn's eyes. Sandy was wearing him down.

"He was all done. Gone bonkers." She circled her finger around her ear. "Crazy."

"What was the medicine for?" I asked.

"Arthritis. He was on Enbrel. It's expensive and he was willing to spend all the money we had saved up to do the soil sample." Her voice cracked. Tears floated on the edges of her lids.

"He was obsessed with growing okra?" Finn's brows furrowed.

"Yes." She turned her chin away from him.

"I also understand that you requested no money from the divorce, but you did ask for the cookbook." I had to look away. If she started crying, it might have an effect on my line of questioning, because I did have a heart. I glanced down at my bag, knowing the very thing she wanted was at my feet.

"Because I was going to destroy it. I loved Owen with everything in my body. But that damn cookbook haunted him. Took his family from him. If it was out of his possession, I figured he'd have no option but to make peace." She looked down at her hands cupped in her lap. "So I served him divorce papers, got a job, and am trying to fix myself up. It makes me feel good. If I didn't, I'd probably had gone back to him."

Finn took over the questioning. "The day he died, you went to court. You lost. Did that make you mad?"

"No. It made me sad." She glared at Finn. "I knew the judge had just killed what was left of him, and I was right."

"What do you mean?" I asked. "Because he was murdered."

She dragged her chin down to her chest. Her head bobbled up and down. Her shoulders slumped. We gave her a minute to compose herself.

"Sandy? Can you answer the question?" I asked again.

"He spent every last dime he had figuring out what was in the soil sample so he could grow his own okra crop. It's expensive, you know." She shook her head. "He couldn't afford to get his meds refilled to keep him from being in crippling pain. It killed him."

"No, he was murdered." Finn uncrossed his legs and scooted his chair back. "And how do we know that you didn't have an argument with him afterward and kill him, knowing Myrna would pretty much cover for you? The two of you could have put him in her greenhouse."

"Why would we do that? Why on earth would I kill him? He had nothing," she said through gritted teeth. "Plus, I certainly wouldn't have put him in my friend's greenhouse."

"You might've wanted the recipe for yourself and the money that came with having some okra in the big organic store." It seemed pretty reasonable coming out of my mouth. "Plus, Myrna is in the cook-off in Cottonwood, which gives her royalties for life. Easy money if she wins."

"I think it's time for you to go." Sandy stood up and pointed toward the front of the house. "I'm not going to let you accuse me of killing Owen without a lawyer present."

"Fine." I pulled a card out of the shirt pocket of my sheriff's uniform. "Tell your lawyer to give me a call."

I walked over to the door we had come in through. I opened

it and pushed the garage-door button. Finn and I left her standing in her kitchen.

"I never leave a house out of a different door from which I entered," I said. "We are going to need all the luck we can get on this case, because there are way more secrets to uncover. Rowdy might have some of those answers."

Chapter Fourteen

On the way back into town, I pulled into the Dixon's Foodtown because I'd been hankering to make the okra recipe from Rae Lynn's cookbook.

"Why don't you come by tonight and we can try our hand at Rae Lynn's okra." I wiggled my brows Finn's way. "I guess we need to see what all the fuss is about."

"I think that's a great idea," Finn agreed.

I left the windows down in the Jeep so Duke could hang out the window and took the composition notebook out of my bag. We walked inside.

"You go grab the cornmeal," I pointed to the recipe and showed him the exact brand Rae Lynn had written down, "while I go grab the okra. Then I'll meet you back in the organic seasoning aisle."

Buying all organic was going to be more expensive, but according to her recipe, we had to use the freshest crop, which in our case was the organic stuff.

The recipe called for the okra to be a half inch in diameter, so I got bigger than that to cut it myself. I grabbed enough to make tonight and, if I really thought I had it down pat, to make for tomorrow's Euchre night with the girls. Finn had also gotten the buttermilk on his way to meet me. I looked at the recipe and grabbed the salt, pepper, and garlic powder.

"You don't have any of these?" Finn asked. I shook my head. "Not even salt?"

"Not even salt." I reached up and grabbed the cayenne pepper and put it in the basket. "I'm telling you, I don't cook."

"You know," he took the basket from me and carried it up to the front, "the way to a man's heart is his stomach."

"I guess I won't be getting any man." My eyes gazed over the checkout lanes, and I went to the farthest one on the right, where there were only two people ahead of us.

"Well, well, well. Look who it is." Toots Buford stuck her hands in her bright red hair, fluffing it up a little more. "How do you do, Officer Finn?" She winked.

"Good today, Ms. Buford. How are you?" he asked. That smile of his could knock any woman off her game.

"I'm doing good now that I've gotten a hello from you." She shimmied her upper body over the conveyor belt.

"What am I? An old dog bone?" I asked, squeezing my way in between Finn and Toots's tits.

"Oh, don't give me that, Kenni Lowry." She pulled back and ran the salt over the scanner. Her eyes drew down to the composition book. "I know what you are up to. I heard all about Owen's death. I know that's his book. The one he and Sandy were fighting over the other day."

"Excuse me?"

My ears perked up.

"That book." She pointed her long red fingernail back over the conveyor, using the other hand to scan the rest of the stuff. "You gonna try your hand at the okra?" She shook the okra in the air before she scanned it. "They could never get it straight."

"When did you see them?" I asked.

"The day he died. They were just getting out of court." The scanner beeped. Her fingers ticked away on the register. "I was just coming on shift when I heard them in the vegetable aisle.

He told her he wasn't giving her that book you have, but he'd be happy to share the recipe with her."

"Anything else? Think," I spat out.

"Kenni, I swear. I try to be nice to you and you never just say, 'thank you, Toots.'" She shook her head. "It will be $25.20."

"You want me to pay you for information?" I snarled.

"Your total is twenty-five dollars and twenty cents." She chomped and folded her arms tightly across her chest.

"Have you had your hair done recently?" Finn leaned on the checkout. Toots smiled and shimmied straight up, popping her chest out.

"I did. Down at Tiny Tina's." She smiled. "You like it?"

"I do." I swear there was a twinkle on his canine tooth. Toots was so busy gushing over him that I had to bag my own groceries.

"Do you mind coming down to the office and giving me a formal statement when you get off work?" He was sweet talking her and she didn't even notice.

She jerked a dangling chain from the front pocket of her jeans and pulled out a heart-shaped Pepé Le Pew pocket watch. "I get off directly." She swiveled her lashes upward.

"I like that pocket watch." Finn toyed with her. She cooed all over herself.

"My mama gave it to me one year for my birthday. She's dead and gone now, but I love it." She leaned across the conveyor, her boobs nearly falling out of her Dixon's shirt and onto the scanner. She gave Finn a good look at them and the watch.

I didn't bother sticking around to listen to the rest.

"She's coming right on down." Finn slammed the door when he got in. "What is it you say around here about vinegar and honey?"

"Forget it," I grumbled and threw the Jeep in gear.

"You could use a little of that honey." He chuckled and stuck his elbow on the window ledge and let it hang out.

"Any woman around here is going to fall for your cute smile and dark eyes." I turned onto Main Street.

"Any woman?" he asked. Duke stuck his head out my window from the backseat.

"If that wasn't proof enough," I said.

"Even you, Sheriff?" he asked. There was no hint of joking in his voice.

I jerked my head and looked at him. There was a smirk on his lips.

"You know what I mean." I rolled my eyes and pulled the Wagoneer down the alley behind Cowboy's.

"You coming in?" Finn asked through the passenger window after he got out and noticed I hadn't.

"No, Casanova, I'll let you handle Toots while I go follow up on Rowdy's call about the stolen flowers, among other questions I have for him." Duke had hopped up to the front seat when Finn got out. I had to push his head to the side to look at Finn.

"Alrighty." He tapped the door with his hand. "I'll see you at the council meeting and then at your place for okra."

I planted the palm of my hand on my forehead. "Dang. I forgot all about the meeting."

"I'm glad you've got me." His head jerked back and a big laugh escaped his belly. "Are you sure I can't charm you too?"

"I'm sure." I pushed the pedal and zoomed off before my smile gave him any ideas.

"There you go again." Poppa appeared in the backseat.

"I'm not dead like you. I can still look even though I know that he's got someone else back in Chicago." I waved to the shop owners on Main Street who were outside of their shops talking to people walking by.

"I told ya. He's just like one of those big-city boys, but he sure does make a damn fine deputy." Poppa was right. Finn was a good deputy, and just because he wasn't interested in me as I thought he might be didn't mean that we couldn't work together.

"Did he tell you about the gal?" Poppa asked.

"Not really." Poppa wasn't going to approve of me snooping. He was always a straight shooter. When he had a question about an investigation, he came right out and asked. I liked to look at all the facts and get those straight before I went around asking any sort of questions.

"Then how do you know?" Poppa's head craned toward his headstone when we pulled in the cemetery.

"I sort of overheard her leave a voicemail for him and then I erased it. Accidentally." The Wagoneer hugged the right of the cemetery road as other cars were parked along the left side. There was a gravesite funeral underneath a big blue tent. In the crowd I saw Rowdy Hart talking with Stanley Godbey.

Stanley looked to be dressed in a suit, which was normal funeral attire around these parts. Rowdy was in his blue work outfit, ready to put the casket in the ground as soon as the preacher gave the last amen. Both men looked my way when they saw me pull over. Rowdy patted Stanley on the back and started to walk toward me.

"Kenni-bug, you have lost your ever-loving mind, and during an election." Poppa stomped around the Wagoneer. "You can't let them see you fold."

"Poppa." I dipped my head to the ground and quickly said to him, "No one knows but you that I erased that message. It's not a big deal. I'm sure Finn has already called her back and their plans are made."

Rowdy waved. "Sheriff, I guess you got my message from Betty." A curse fell from his mouth. "I'm sorry to be disrespectful, but what kind of jerk goes around stealing flowers off a dead man's grave?"

"I have no idea. But I agree that it's very tacky." I pulled my notebook out of my Jeep and headed over to him. "What can you tell me about Owen Godbey?"

I had decided to take Poppa's approach to questioning.

"Kenni?" His nostrils flared. "Did you hear what I said about them flowers?"

His anger caught me off guard. There was a shift in his personality that I'd never seen before.

"I sure did." I nodded and tried not to look at Stanley when he walked up. "I have to make sure that the flowers that are missing have nothing to do with Owen since he was found in a greenhouse tied to most of the flowers here."

"Are you saying you do suspect Myrna Savage in the murder of my brother?" Stanley jerked with a quick snap of his thick shoulders. He put his hands in the pockets of his suit pants.

"I'm not saying who is and isn't a suspect." I eyed him and took the cop stance with my legs apart and arms clasped behind me. The academy taught us that particular stance exuded authority. "But I do know that Rowdy gave Owen a job around the cemetery and now the flowers are missing." I turned back to Rowdy. "Do you know if Owen had anything to do with the flowers that were missing? Did they come from Myrna? If so, was Owen so mad at Myrna that he went around and destroyed or took off all the Petal Pusher arrangements and you are just now noticing?"

"That's a good question. I never thought of it that way." Rowdy dragged the old blue baseball cap off his head and gave his noggin a good scratch. "But he was so arthritic that he..." Rowdy paused. His eyes gazed over the tops of the gravestones before he brought his attention back to me. "Sheriff, can I take a rain check?"

"I'm sorry?" I asked.

"I need to tend to some business and I want to check something out before I go accusing the dead of stealing. It ain't right by me or Owen," he said. He put his cap back on his head and hooked his thumbs in the front pockets of his blue jumpsuit. "Besides, I have a casket to get in the ground and another grave to start digging."

We stepped aside to let the mourners who were there for the funeral drive past us.

"Why don't you come by the office tomorrow morning before work and we can talk about it." There was no sense in asking him questions here while I could take his statement at the office without Stanley Godbey listening in.

"I'm assuming you are going to keep me up to date on what's going on with the investigation." Stanley cleared his throat, lifted his head, and looked down his nose at me.

I glared at him and ignored his request. "I wanted to let you know that Sandy will be picking up Owen's remains and she will be in charge of the arrangements for him since she and Owen had prearranged plans at Cottonwood Funeral Home."

"She can't do that." There was bridled anger in his voice. "They are divorced and she only wanted him because of the..." He pinched his lips together.

"Only wanted him because of this?" I jerked open the door of the Wagoneer and pulled the composition book out of my bag, holding it up in front of me.

"Where did you get that?" Stanley took a step forward. His large hand swiped the air just as I pulled it back.

"I wouldn't do that if I were you." I had a much stronger guard up now. "This is being processed as evidence."

"My mother's cookbook?" he questioned.

"You wouldn't believe how the smallest of things help solve crimes." I held the book tight to my chest with one hand and rested my other hand on my gun holster, trying to read his body language. "I haven't let this baby get out of my sight since I found it. Just in case you know who ransacked my house and stuck a knife in the front seat of my Jeep, let them know that I'm on to them and they will not get this."

"Sounds to me like you need to make your own police report." Stanley glared.

"Is there something you'd like to tell me? Something you need to get off your chest?" I asked.

"Are you accusing me of breaking into your house, Sheriff?" he asked with a smug look on his face. His mouth opened. His eyes bore deep in my soul. He ran his tongue along the tops of his teeth before he shut his lips.

He lifted his hand in the air as if he was going to backhand me. It took everything in me not to flinch. I gripped the butt of my gun that was snapped in my holster.

His eyes shifted.

At that moment, I had to wonder if he abused Inez. I'd seen the way he treated her when I went to his house to tell them about Owen and her reaction when I took her home from craft night. It sure did resemble that of a scared woman.

He stuck his pointer finger at me. "I hope you come to the council meeting tonight."

We stood there a minute too long before he blinked first and started to walk past me, nearly taking my rotator cuff with him.

Duke went wild from inside the Wagoneer when he saw Stanley bump into me. "Mangy mutt," he muttered.

"Stay." I ordered Duke, knowing that if he really wanted to, he could jump out the window and take Stanley down in a minute.

"That was good." Poppa's voice came from behind me.

I continued to watch Stanley Godbey walk to his truck with a stalking, purposeful intent.

I whispered, "I figured I would take a lesson from your book and lay a few of my cards out on the table. If Stanley did kill his brother, he will be on high alert since he knows I'm watching. He will mess up. They all do in time."

"Time we have. Owen is already dead and he ain't going nowhere fast. Neither are we." Poppa rubbed his hands together briskly. Excitement escalated in his voice. "Neither are we."

I hated to admit it, but Stanley suggesting I be at the council meeting got my curiosity up. Of course I was going, but I had no idea what was on the docket except my plan to introduce the idea that the sheriff's department needed our own building, not the rented storage space in the back of Cowboy's Catfish.

Chapter Fifteen

"S&S Auto Salvage." I could picture that woman behind her desk that was so kind and sweet until she knew why I'd come to her place of business. "How can I help you?"

"This is Sheriff Lowry from Cottonwood. I was there the other day with my partner picking up a truck that y'all had towed in." I paused, waiting for her to acknowledge me, but when there was dead air between us, I continued, "I had driven the truck back to the station in Cottonwood and left my Wagoneer in your parking lot. When I picked it up later, someone had broken into it and stuck a knife in my passenger side seat with a somewhat threatening message." I paused again. Nothing. So I said, "I noticed you have security cameras on the building and I'm going to come by for the feed. Now, do you need me to get a warrant or can I just have it? Because messing with an official police vehicle leads to jail time."

"You can't do either," she said matter-of-factly.

"Did you not understand the jail part?" I questioned the phone connection. After all, I was on a cell phone traveling through my small town on the way to Hart Insurance and service was spotty.

"I heard you perfectly, Sheriff. Those cameras don't have a feed. We have them there like people put up the security-company signs in their yard. Just to deter," she said firmly. "So if there isn't anything else I can do for you today, then I have got to go."

"I'll be in touch," I said.

"I bet you will." Her voice, deep with sarcasm, was followed up by a slam of her phone receiver.

"Oh, Duke." I looked over at my pooch. His head was hung out the window and his tongue was flapping slobber all over the windshield.

I parked the Jeep in the open parking space right in front of Hart Insurance.

"Let's go." I patted my leg for Duke to follow.

Katy Lee Hart was on the phone with a customer when we walked in. Duke laid down in front of the air vent, and I thumbed through the racks of Shabby Trends, the clothing line that Katy Lee sold on the side. It was kinda like Tupperware, only with clothes.

"Spill it," I said when she hung up. I took a look at a dress and then pushed the hanger to the left. "What is on the council meeting docket tonight?"

"How would I know?" She moved to one of the leather couches in the lobby of Hart Insurance, where she ran the family business. She pulled her blond hair over her shoulder, letting it fall down into curly tendrils.

Katy Lee and I had been friends since grade school. She was always a good person to talk to.

"Stanley Godbey said something to me over at the cemetery when I was visiting your brother." I picked up a hanger with a short-sleeved black blouse that had the shoulders cut out of it but still had sleeves. I'd seen the design in some of the magazines I perused while waiting in line at Dixon's. "This is cute."

I held it up to me and looked in the front window of the insurance shop that was located in a strip mall.

"Big seller." Katy Lee stood up and plucked a pair of white jeans off the rack. "This is really cute together." She handed it me. "Go try it on in the bathroom."

I took the clothes and went into the bathroom.

"So you have nothing to add to the docket tonight?" I asked.

"If you're fishing for new properties that came up, I just might have one on the south side just outside of city limits that used to be the old Day's car lot." Her voice was a little louder so I could hear her through the closed bathroom door. "You know the property that has a big chain-link fence around it and the cement building with three rooms plus an office that would make a great office for a sheriff's department."

"You're joking." I flung the door open, the jeans barely up around my hiney. I jerked up the zipper, not caring a bit about the outfit. "That's the first thing you should've told me when I walked in the door instead of 'here, look through the latest line of Shabby Trends.'" I caught my reflection in the window and twisted around to see what my butt looked like in the jeans. "Oh, cute."

"Super cute. He's going to love it." Katy Lee bounced on her toes.

"Who?" I asked.

"One hunky deputy named Finn Vincent." She giggled. "Toots Buford told everyone that you were in there today getting all sorts of ingredients and spices to cook. I just knew they were wrong because the Kendrick Lowry I know has never cooked, much less knows how to turn a stove on." She pursed her lips and gave me the stink eye. "Now, that is what you should've told me about when you walked into this office."

"Touché." I smiled. "I am going to try to cook, but it's for an experiment with Owen's recipe, not a date."

"Why, I don't see why not." Katy Lee walked over and ran her fingers along the cutout of the sleeves and poked and prodded me. "He doesn't have to know it's a date. A little cooking here, flirting there, kissing." She made smoochie noises.

"He's got a girlfriend." I shook my head. "Even though he told me he didn't."

I didn't go into details about the Ferris wheel and how he'd told me the photo was his sister.

"Then how do you know he has one?" Katy Lee walked over to her desk and picked up a file.

"Oh God, Katy Lee. I lost my mind last night." I quickly told her about how I had gone to grab the pie and my fingers took over my body and hit the erase button on his machine.

Katy Lee was laughing so hard she snorted, causing a laugh to ripple through me. I swear we laughed for ten minutes until we were practically crying.

"I thought those games ended when we were in high school." Katy Lee handed a folder over to me. "But I guess we feel love as if we were still teenagers."

"I'm not loving anyone. Especially Finn Vincent." I tried to cover any sort of feelings I had with a low chuckle. The tab on the folder read "Day's Auto"—the specs for the potential office building. "Thanks."

"Since you told me you've been looking for a bigger place and wanted to get that as part of your platform for re-election, I've kept my nose to the ground. I really think this property is perfect. I even asked Doolittle Bowman about the budget that'd been set aside for years for a new sheriff's office and it is totally in budget. I put the numbers in there so you can present it tonight."

"You're a good friend." I smiled. "I've got to get out of these clothes and get out of here."

I had just enough time to get Duke home and head back to Luke Jones's house, where the town council held the city meetings.

"Keep them." She practically pushed me out the door. "Keep them on so when you are cooking, you can at least give him something to look at." She winked and shut the door behind me.

"This here just might be our ticket to re-election," I told Duke when I got back in the Jeep. He didn't bother picking his head up to acknowledge me.

As the Wagoneer rolled down Main Street on our way to Free Row, Duke popped up with his paws on the ledge and big ears flopping around while his tongue stuck out of the side of his mouth.

I was happy to find my house all in one piece. I put away my sheriff's things and took another look at myself in the mirror before I swiped on some lipstick and ran a brush through my hair. Katy Lee was right. The outfit was adorable. It was a shame that I was going to waste it by trying to fry some okra.

"You be a good boy."

I put a scoop of kibble in Duke's bowl and headed on out the door.

The council meeting would fill up fast and I wanted to make sure I got there and greeted everyone. Like Bartleby Fry said, it would be election time soon and I was going to have to shake hands and hold babies. Plus help the Sweet Adelines to their seats, though I was sure Mama had already threatened them within an inch of their lives if they didn't vote for me.

It was a hard spot for my mama. She didn't like the idea of her daughter being sheriff and in somewhat dangerous situations, but she didn't like to lose either. And that meant that no matter what, she'd walk the streets and knock on every single door and not leave until they swore on the good man above that I had their vote. Gotta love a good southern mama like my own.

The street out front of Luke and Vita Jones's house was lined with people on both sides. It was great to see that the community came out to the council meetings even though they were held in a basement.

Luke was an entrepreneur of sorts. He owned the Pump and Munch filling station in the middle of town, where he was the mechanic as well as the cashier of the mini-mart inside. It was a good place to go if you only needed to pick up a few items. Other than that, everyone went to Dixon's to grocery shop.

Luke also ran the movie theatre in Cottonwood, which also happened to be in the basement of his house. He loved movies and most nights he'd invite half the town over to watch, so when he and Vita bought this house, he decided to turn the big basement into a movie theatre with a pull-down screen and even a popcorn maker. Most nights Vita stood in the back making all the popcorn and handing out Cokes.

From the looks of the posters hanging on the wall inside, Luke was showing romantic comedies—*Sweet Home Alabama* was this week's feature.

"Let's come to order." Mayor Ryland banged the gavel on the podium at the front of the room. The rows of folding chairs were filled and it was standing room only. "Order!"

Mayor Ryland was in his sixties. He was very debonair with freshly dyed black hair that he slicked back. He had a strong jaw that even his goatee couldn't hide.

"Shut up, everyone." Doolittle Bowman stood up and tried to calm the crowd. She didn't mind taking over. She was good at it. She was the county clerk and always had her nose in everyone's business.

The room quieted down and the council went over all the regular business and the fiscal calendar, as well as the budget and how everyone was on plan. All the regulars were there except Rowdy Hart. He was generally the one who set up the chairs for Luke.

"Where's Rowdy?" I asked Vita, who was next to me.

She shrugged. "He never showed."

A strange nervous unease came over me. I couldn't recall a meeting where Rowdy wasn't there. I looked forward to him coming by the office tomorrow to find out exactly where he was.

"Is there any other order of business?" Mayor Ryland asked.

I pushed off the back wall and put my hand in the air to be called on. I couldn't wait to propose the new sheriff's office site, knowing it'd been a long time coming.

"Stanley Godbey."

The mayor skipped me and called Stanley up to the podium.

"This should be good," Poppa mumbled from next to me. I tried not to look at him and bring any attention to myself.

"Mayor, council members." Stanley's eyes scanned the room and stopped when our eyes locked. "Sheriff." He nodded.

My gut told me to hold on. Something was about to go down.

"It's come to my attention that there has been a slew of break-ins, thefts, and murders in Cottonwood. I, not only as a citizen, but as a beloved brother to one of those murder victims, feel unsafe in the very place I lay my head." Stanley wasn't fooling anyone. His words were thrown at me like a dart. And they were meant to hurt. "Now, when Sheriff Sims was alive, God bless his soul, he was able to keep crime at a minimum. He kept me and my Inez safe. We were able to go to sleep and not worry about our crop."

He made a hand gesture to Luke Jones. Luke flipped a switch and the movie screen scrolled down.

"As you can see in this video footage, someone keeps getting into my crops. Clearly on the second night of the week, you can see someone with the same build and size as the first night. You all know that no one can make an okra crop like my mama, Rae Lynn." He frowned. "I know Mama and Sheriff Sims are in heaven right now eating some of her good fried okra."

"Don't you bring Rae Lynn into this," Poppa warned, his fist in the air as if he was going to give Stanley a good pop in the kisser. "Kenni, stop this man right now."

I bit my tongue and kept my ears open. I also couldn't help but notice that the okra crop didn't seem to be healthy looking. It was droopy and dry.

"After the last rash of crimes that hit Cottonwood, I had to put in a security camera just so me and my sweet Inez could get some sort of shut eye." The video of someone sneaking into their crop fields played over and over. It was so grainy that you could only make out two legs running up to the crop and then leaving. "I can deal with someone trying to come in and steal whatever they are trying to take from the okra crop since I don't farm it anymore, but I will not stand here and let people break into our own homes just like someone did in our own Sheriff Lowry's home." He pointed his finger at me and shook it with a passion.

A collective gasp blanketed the room and the chair legs squeaked when everyone turned around to look at me.

"If she can't keep her own home safe, how is she going to keep our community safe?" he asked. There was some scattered applause. His voice escalated over the crowd like one of the evangelical preachers you see on the television when they are building up for an uproar in the audience. "It's almost time for election season to begin, and I don't know about you, but I want to bring our safe community back and the only way we can do that is for Lonnie Lemar to come out of retirement and run for sheriff."

"Sit your ass down!" my mama screamed from the front row. "Right now, Stanley Godbey. Rae Lynn would be ashamed of you." Mama wasn't above shaming anyone in public.

Daddy put his arm around Mama and pulled her up to

standing. I thought she was going to faint then and there. He grabbed her by the shoulders and ushered her out of Luke's basement. We glanced at each other as they passed, Daddy giving me a sympathetic look while Mama had her head buried in his shoulder.

"Now I don't mean no disrespect to Sheriff Lowry, but I do think we need someone with a proven track record that'd helped keep us safe. That's why I am announcing that Lonnie Lemar is officially coming out of retirement." Out of nowhere, Lonnie jumped up on stage with his arms spread wide open and a big grin on his old wrinkly face.

I looked down to make sure I had on those white pants. Because about right now, I felt like I'd been caught with my pants down.

Chapter Sixteen

"Lonnie is about as useless as a screen door on a submarine, Kenni-bug." Poppa tried to talk me down on my way home. "He can't hold a candle to you. He's too old to take on Cottonwood."

"Maybe, but he sure is going to try." I was gripping the steering wheel so hard, I could feel my heartbeat pulse in my fingertips. "It's more important now than ever to bring Owen's killer to justice. Earlier I thought we had some time, but now I'm not so sure."

"What did you make of the video footage?" Poppa asked.

"Not much. According to Sandy, Owen had snuck over to Stanley's and got a soil sample. Apparently it's pretty expensive to get one of those analyzed and Owen used all his money to have it done and that was all he had left for his arthritis meds."

"Something is missing. A key ingredient." Poppa reached over and tapped the cookbook that I never let leave my sight. "Stanley sure did hit below the belt when he said something about someone breaking in your house."

"He made me look incompetent." That angered me more than him wanting someone to run against me. "Trust me, if I were home when they tried that, they'd have had a bullet in their foot."

Finn's Charger was sitting by the curb outside of my house when we pulled up. He was leaning up against the hood in his fancy jeans with the stylish rips in them and a gray V-neck t-shirt. He was on the phone and smiling while talking.

That was just another turn of the knife put in my back by Stanley.

"I've got to go. I'll see you tomorrow," he told the other person as I walked up.

"Where're you going tomorrow?" I asked. I held the cookbook and the folder Katy Lee had given me.

"You gave me the weekend off to go back to Chicago, remember?" He tilted his head and looked at me all confused. "You look nice."

"That was before there was a murdered Owen Godbey found and we have no one in custody." I glared at him, knowing that my anger was stemming from a lot of things. At the moment it was mostly the fear of me losing my job to crotchety old Lonnie Lemar.

"Is something going on?" Finn pushed himself up to his feet. "Because if there is, I can go home and start packing for my weekend. I thought it would be fun to try to cook the recipe and see what all the fuss was about."

"No. I'm sorry." The last thing I needed to was to be all alone. "I went to the council meeting to propose a new site for a sheriff's office." I held up the file.

"Very cool. I'll look at it inside." He reached into the Charger and pulled out a bottle of red wine. "To complement the okra. Toots gave it to me when she came by to give her statement."

"Kenni," Poppa warned. "You can't do wine."

"Great." I grabbed the bottle. "I'll get us a couple glasses. Come on."

Duke had already jumped the fence in the backyard and ran around.

"What's the purpose of the fence if he can jump it?" Finn

looked out the kitchen window while I poured the wine. He dug his hands into the Dixon's bag and took out all the ingredients we'd bought earlier before the meeting.

"To keep the outside world out." I handed him a glass. Our fingers touched and lingered.

"You do look nice." He pulled away first. "I don't think I've seen you in anything other than the brown uniform or jeans and a sweatshirt."

"So you don't find me disturbingly attractive in my everyday clothes?" I imagined his girlfriend in a black lace nightie, flowing black hair pulled over her shoulder, her long and lean nicely waxed tan legs probably a mile long as she lounged on his bed back in Chicago.

"Prettiest sheriff I know." He clapped his hands. "Now, where is that cookbook?"

It was obvious that I'd made him uncomfortable by crossing the line. I was fully aware of his masculinity under that tee. He ran his finger down the ingredients and read them out loud. I didn't hear a single thing. My eyes were focused on his bicep that seemed firm without him even flexing.

"Don't you think?" he asked, turning around. "Kenni?"

"Yep." I came out of my Finn coma and took a big gulp of wine.

"Did you hear what I said?" he asked and continued to cut the okra per the instructions.

"Yeah. Umm...no." I shook my head and took another big gulp.

"I said that Sandy and Owen were a lot chummier than we thought, according to Toots."

"According to Toots, we are having a date." My pinkie finger gestured between us, the stem of the wineglass held with my other fingers. I took another drink. "Toots is wrong. Way wrong."

"Is she?" he asked and looked over his shoulder, the knife up in the air.

"I don't know if she is or not." I picked up the wine bottle and poured myself a very generous glass because I wasn't sure if he was referring to Toots being wrong about Sandy and Owen or if he meant this was a date. I decided to put my strange feelings aside and chalk up his question about Toots to be about Sandy and Owen. "You saw Sandy's reaction when she talked about Owen. She was angry about how he used all the money for the soil report."

"Which I did look up online while I was waiting for Toots." He ran his finger down the recipe while I got the cast-iron skillet ready for the frying. "I made a few calls to labs that do specific soil treatment. I found the one Owen sent his sample to. They received it twelve days ago and it takes at least two weeks to get it back. They are going to fax the sample results to me when they are completed."

"You got all of that information through a phone call?" I asked. We both knew that in order to get results from a lab, a warrant was usually involved.

"A little sweet talking never hurt anyone." He dipped the cut okra into the buttermilk like Rae Lynn's recipe called for before he dredged it in the cornmeal, cayenne pepper, flour, salt, black pepper, and garlic mix that I'd combined in a bowl. "I wonder what this means." He read from the book, "Continue using the seeds from the very first plant in the first row for each new harvest before you till the old."

I shrugged and took another drink.

"Maybe you can sweet talk Stanley Godbey into thinking I am a good sheriff and that there's no need for Lonnie to come out of retirement to run against me." The wine was starting to make me a little light headed.

Finn checked the hot skillet by flicking a drop of water into it and watched it sizzle. I continue to wash and cut ends off of more okra before cutting it into four pieces and dragging it into the breaded mix.

"What?" Finn carefully added the breaded okra into the hot skillet. "Lonnie Lemar?"

I held the glass up and tilted it Finn's way before I took another gulp. "Before I could even propose the new building for our office, Stanley Godbey took the floor during the open docket and told everyone that since I took office, the crime rate has shot up and a new sheriff is in order. Suddenly Lonnie appeared out of nowhere and Stanley announced Lonnie was coming out of retirement to run for sheriff in the election."

"Isn't he pretty old though? I mean to want to run for sheriff?" Finn asked and used the tongs to take the fried okra pieces out of the skillet.

"I just can't believe that Lonnie would even listen to Stanley." I shook my head. "That low-down dirty sonofa..." I slurred my words as the anger and wine bubbled up in me.

"I think you've had enough to drink." Finn sucked in a deep breath. "We're working on finding out what is so special about this okra."

"What? This isn't a date?" I smiled and pretended to joke, losing my balance when I took a step backwards.

"Okay." Finn grabbed me before I went down to the ground and stuck me in the kitchen chair. "You stay while I finish this up. Then we will have you sobered up in no time."

"I told you not to have the wine." Poppa leaned up against the table.

Duke ran over with his ball in his mouth and dropped it at Poppa's feet. He barked at Poppa.

"He's going to keep barking until you throw it," I said to Poppa. "Duke, Poppa doesn't want to play. He's mad that I'm drinking wine."

"Are you okay?" Finn walked over and kicked the tennis ball from underneath the table, sending Duke off in a frenzy after it.

"I'm fine." I waved my hand in the air before my head smacked the table.

Chapter Seventeen

"Oh, Duke." I pushed the big lug off me on the first snooze alarm. Then my memory kicked in that if I didn't drag myself out of bed, I'd have a big puddle of pee to clean up. "Oh, Duke!"

I jumped out of bed, only to have to steady myself from the gonging in my head.

"Oh no," I groaned and rubbed my head. I stumbled down the hall into the kitchen and opened up the back door before Duke could relieve himself on the kitchen floor. "Coffee."

I eyed the sticky note on the coffee pot.

"Coffee already made for you. Just turn it on," Finn had written on it. "Good morning. Take two aspirin and don't worry about Lonnie Lemar." I flipped the switch on.

A smile flooded my entire face, my cheeks balled. I couldn't deny that I liked spending time alone with Finn, even if it was drowning my sorrows in wine, and even if he did have a girlfriend.

"Yep. I told you not to drink wine." Poppa sat in a chair at the table. "You couldn't even taste the okra that boy made because you passed out." The shame was written all over Poppa's face. "I even started to like him because he took nice care of you."

"Now you like him, after I find out he's taken." I eyed the fried okra Finn'd made and left on a plate sitting on top of the stove. The coffee pot was only half brewed, but I had to have a jolt. Finn had even put a mug next to the pot along with the aspirin.

After a couple of pieces of the okra, I took a nice long sip of the piping hot coffee.

The strong coffee steam floated up in the air and curled around my nose as I tipped the cup, instantly making me feel better. I popped the pills in my mouth and took another sip of coffee. It was so good, my eyes closed automatically from the pure satisfaction.

"At first when he picked you up and took you back to your bedroom, I was thinking he was going to take advantage of you." Duke scratched at the door and I let him in. He immediately ran over to Poppa's feet and sat down, staring up at him. "Then he put you on the bed and took the quilt off the quilt rack. He said something about Chicago and you and his life."

"What?" I asked, hurrying over to the table with the cup and plate of okra. "What did he say about Chicago?" I shivered, recalling that he was going to Chicago this morning and was going to be spending time with the woman on the other end of his answering machine.

"I wasn't listening to him. I was busy trying to pick up that framed picture of me and you sitting on your dresser so I could wing it at him when he tried to get fresh with you." Poppa never liked it when I had a boyfriend. "Just so you know, that movie *Ghost* where the ghost can pick up the penny? Well, that's not real-life ghosting."

"Thank you for making that clear." I smiled at Poppa and devoured some more fried okra. "You thought *MacGyver* was real too." I referred to the television show he loved to watch when I was a kid. Poppa talked to the television as though he was right alongside MacGyver solving crimes.

"Anyways, that boy tucked you into the quilt and patted the

side of the bed and told Duke to stay and keep you safe." Poppa smiled.

"Are you smiling at the image of Finn tucking me in?" I teased.

"I'm thinking I can show up in Chicago and scare that girl off, because he just might be good for you." Poppa disappeared.

"Don't you dare!" I shouted out into the air. After a moment without him showing back up, I shrugged and ate the last few pieces of okra. "Dang, that was good okra."

"Don't you dare what?" Mrs. Brown, my neighbor, stood at the screen door. She shuffled inside and patted a very excited Duke. "What did I hear you say about some okra?"

"Duke was trying to drink my coffee." *Coffee? What is wrong with me?*

"You like coffee?" Mrs. Brown asked Duke in a baby voice. Duke wagged his tail and sniffed the pocket on her apron. Her hair was rolled tight in pink sponge curlers underneath a hair cap. "Well, I'm not giving you any coffee or okra today." She pulled a dog biscuit out of the pocket.

"Mrs. Brown, what's going on?" I asked, wondering why she was here.

"I'm here because of this." She handed me a sticky note. She tugged on a sponge curler sticking out and a perfect curl sprang up.

It was from Finn. He'd asked her to take care of Duke for me today. Duke was used to Mrs. Brown. On days I knew I was going to be gone for a long time or had things to do where Duke couldn't come, she always let him out and fed him for me.

"I found it on my front door this morning." She shuffled over to the table and eased down. "I'll take a cup of coffee."

"Where are my manners?" I grabbed a mug out of the cabinet and poured her a steaming cup. It was the least I could do since I had accidentally pulled a loaded pistol on her a few weeks ago when I came home and thought she was an intruder when she was actually just letting Duke out. "Thank you. Finn is out of town today and I have to be a lot of places. He must've known I needed someone to take care of Duke."

"He is a hunk." She winked and blew on the coffee before she took a sip. I sat across the table from her. "And someone is going to snatch him up if you don't watch it. Now I told Polly to dump that old man because at his age I'm sure he can't get it—"

"Enough." I put my hand up. Polly Parker was Mrs. Brown's niece and Polly just so happened to be in her twenties and dating Mayor Ryland, who was a good thirty years older than her. I sure didn't want to know anything about their private life.

I had uncovered their love affair during one of my investigations and the community was horrified. Now that some time had passed, they were no longer the center of gossip. Apparently Finn and I had taken that spot.

"You are young and so is he. Take it from an old woman, enjoy your life. And by that, I mean sex." She reached across the table and patted my hand. "I heard what happened last night at the council meeting."

"Please stop," I begged. "Owen Godbey is taking up all my time and if I don't hurry up and solve this murder, what you heard about the council meeting just might happen."

"No, it won't. Your mama won't let anyone win against you." She used her curled fists to help her stand up before I could get around the table to help. "You ready, Duke?"

Duke ran to the door and wagged his tail, panting with anticipation.

"Not too many treats today," I said when I held open the door for them.

"I can't promise nothing." Mrs. Brown shuffled out the door with Duke next to her.

I shut the door and leaned up against it. Finn had me all

confused. Why on earth would he do something so sweet like tuck me in? Or take the time to make my coffee? Or even go to Mrs. Brown's and ask her to take care of Duke because he knew he wasn't going to be here to help me with the investigation and Duke was just another thing off my plate? Why do all that when he had a girlfriend?

Not that all of these things were boyfriend-type things, but they certainly weren't the usual activities of a deputy sheriff.

The calendar alarm on my phone chirped from my bedroom, reminding me to get to the office on time to meet Rowdy Hart.

I quickly showered, put my uniform on, and pinned my poppa's sheriff pin on my lapel. I headed to the office for my interview with Rowdy. I was curious to see what he had to tell me that he couldn't yesterday when I went to the cemetery.

"Good morning." Betty said from her desk when I walked in.

"Good morning." On my way over to my desk I checked the fax machine to see if the lab had faxed over any new results from the evidence we'd sent in. A strange feeling swept over me when I looked over at Finn's empty desk. It reminded me to send him a quick text and thank him for last night.

"I hear you tied one on last night after the council meeting." Betty's accusing eyes stared me down. She was judging me.

"Finn has a big mouth." My brows lifted.

"Not Finn." Her eyes lowered. Yep, she was definitely judging me. "Mrs. Brown and I had a little chat this morning when she called dispatch all worried about what she'd heard about the town-council meeting."

In a small town like Cottonwood and with Betty Murphy at the dispatch line, everyone called her to get the scoop on what was going on around town since they assumed the sheriff's office knew everything.

"No need to worry." I played off the idea that Lonnie would beat me in an election.

"I wouldn't be so sure." She held something up in the air. "This was stuck in my door when I left this morning."

"'Lonnie is LOYAL to keeping Cottonwood safe,'" I read the bumper sticker with a snarled nose. "Who left it there?"

"I have no idea." She shrugged. "But they are getting an early start. And we are months away from the election."

"Years," I grumbled. Lonnie was the last person I needed grief from right now.

I crumpled the bumper sticker up in my fist and threw it in the wastebasket. I glanced up at the clock and noticed it was past time for Rowdy to be here and wondered if he forgot.

"Did Rowdy Hart call?" I asked Betty.

"Not a word." She shook her head. "You expecting him to?"

"Yes. Yesterday I went by the cemetery to talk to him about the stolen flowers and he said he wanted to talk to me alone." The look on his face tormented my mind. "I told him to meet me here first thing." I glanced up at the clock.

It was strange for him not to show up. In fact, Rowdy Hart was always too early for everything.

"He wasn't at the council meeting last night either." There was a stabbing feeling of uneasiness in my gut.

"I'm sure he'll turn up directly." Betty drew her lips into a tight smile.

"I hope you're right, or I'm going to have to go looking for him." The door opened and in sashayed my mama.

"There you are." Mama stomped through the door with a great big smile on her face. "I've been all over looking for you."

"And by all over what do you mean?" I asked, because there were few places I frequented.

"On The Run. Your house. Here." Mama trotted over. She handed me a plastic five-point-star sheriff's pin that read "Re-elect Sheriff Lowry" like the ones she had stuck up and down the lapel of her blue pantsuit.

"What are those?" My jaw dropped. My face reddened. "Who has seen these?"

"Everyone I have walked by this morning." She put her hands on her hips and swung her leg to the side. "I about had to take to the bed last night when Stanley got up on that stage and gossiped about our family." She rolled back her shoulders and stuck her chin in the air. "But you know what I said?"

"No, Mama. What?" I didn't know why I encouraged her, but the entertainment factor might help my mood.

"I said, listen here, you can either lay down like a dog or you can jump up like a gazelle." She leaned over and pinned a re-election pin next to my badge. "I chose gazelle."

"Do you even know what a gazelle looks like?" I asked.

"Of course, I watch the National Geographic channel. I'm a gazelle and you are not going to let Lonnie Lemar, who just so happens to be a sloth, get a leg up on you." Her brows wiggled. "We," she gestured between me and her, "are gazelles."

Somehow I couldn't picture Mama as a gazelle.

"I happen to think sloths are cute." Which they were. "And I'm not too concerned about being re-elected. Stanley Godbey is just upset about Owen. He wants me to solve the murder yesterday when he has no idea just how much work goes into it."

"Here." She slapped a bag full of Re-elect Lowry pins on my desk. "While you are out and about today, you hand these out after you kiss all the babies you see." She turned. "Bye, Betty. I'll see you at Euchre." She stopped shy of the door. "I'll see you too, Kenni."

She waved her fingers in the air and was gone.

"Oh man."

I had totally forgotten about Euchre tonight. It would be a great distraction from me thinking about what Finn might be doing with that woman in Chicago—but it would take time away from the investigation.

"Betty," I put the bag of pins on her desk, "I'm going to the cemetery to see Rowdy. He must've either forgotten or is running late this morning."

"I'll hold down the fort." She waved and pulled out some fingernail polish and shook the bottle as I walked out. "And I'll hand out those pins over at Cowboy's when I go over there to get my iced tea."

There was a crowd gathered around the *Cottonwood Chronicle* box on the corner of the alley. Everyone was in line to put in their quarter to get a look at what Edna Easterly had printed. I rubbernecked to get a look at the front-page headlines as I brought the Jeep to a stop at the red light. Poppa stood behind a couple of people who were pointing and discussing the feature article on the front page.

"'Catfight' written in bold red print right across the top." Poppa appeared next to me. "There is a picture of Myrna and Inez going at it at Lulu's Boutique and you are standing in the background looking at them."

Damn Edna Easterly, my mind spat. "Why on earth would Edna print that?" I couldn't wrap my brain around it.

"She's keeping the public aware of what's going on," Poppa said. But he and I both knew she was only stirring up trouble.

"She's making the public afraid, which isn't going to help with my re-election. If the citizens of Cottonwood don't feel safe under my authority, I'm done for." I gripped the wheel and took off when the light turned green. "Did you read any of the article?" I asked, trying to satisfy my curiosity.

He fidgeted in the seat like there were ants crawling all over him.

"What?" I asked and continued through town, going north toward the cemetery. "Tell me."

"You aren't going to like it, especially since you have Edna working for you."

Something flickered in Poppa's eyes.

"Tell me." My voice was tight and so was my throat.

"Stanley is interviewed in the article. Apparently, Edna showed him the photos and he gave a statement about the event according to his wife."

I looked over at Poppa and caught an unexpected concerned look on his face.

"He also told them how you had left your sheriff's bag unattended and Inez got a look inside, where you had your gun and holster with your Taser tucked in there, making it look like you're sloppy with your work." Poppa paused like he was chewing on the words that he was about to spit out.

"Go on. I'm a big girl." I wasn't going to lie. It didn't feel good to have an entire article make you sound like an imbecile and question your character and even your work ethic. Truth was that Stanley was right. I did leave the bag there and it was a big mistake.

"He went on to say that the crime rate has gone up 100 percent." Poppa's voice cracked. "I'm sorry, Kenni-bug."

"Why are you sorry?" I acted as though I was paying a lot more attention to driving through the cemetery than I really was.

"I honestly thought scaring off all the would-be crimes over the past few years would help you, keep you safe, but now it's backfired and I've put more of a target on your back, only it's from the citizens who should be supporting you." Poppa disappeared.

"Wait." I slammed on the brakes of the Wagoneer, bringing it to a screeching halt. "I love you being here and this has nothing to do with you or me. It has everything to do with Owen." My voice trailed off when I realized Poppa was gone. "If

I had to choose between being sheriff and being haunted by you, I'd pick you every time."

"That's what I'm afraid of," Poppa's voice answered, though I couldn't see him. "If you didn't need me, I might not have a purpose to be here. So we've got to find the killer and stop Stanley Godbey's campaign against you."

Stanley Godbey was a thorn in my side. Thorns were meant to be pulled out. Stanley wasn't going to bother me much longer. I was sure Rowdy had some answers that I was looking for.

The city truck Rowdy drove was parked in the new section of the cemetery that had just been cultivated for new plots. The driver's door of his truck was open. There was a shovel stuck in the ground next to a pile of dirt where it looked like he had been digging a grave.

I pulled up behind his truck and parked. The sun was already coming out and the fresh air from such a peaceful place filled my lungs. The deep inhale and exhale of the air made the cobwebs in my brain from the night before seem to clear. My body was beginning to feel normal again. Poppa was right. I wasn't able to drink wine. Aside from a next-day headache, it always made me tipsier or downright drunker than even moonshine.

"Rowdy?" I called when I didn't see any sign of him. "Rowdy, you hand-digging graves now?" I yelled even louder and walked over to the hole and looked down.

A blood-curdling scream started from the bottom of my feet straight up through my body, leaving me shaking in my sheriff's shoes.

Chapter Eighteen

"I'm so glad you decided it wasn't the right time to leave." My temples began to throb. Finn and I stood there as Max wheeled Rowdy's body into the hearse. My legs felt spongy. I shook my head to clear my thoughts. I couldn't believe Rowdy would commit suicide.

I was shocked to see Finn drive up as I was securing the scene and taking bullet fragments, soil samples from the shoe prints in the freshly dug dirt, and photos of the crime scene. The fragments from the bullet would help the lab and Max determine the distance of the gun—if it was close up for a suicide or farther away. The trace metals would also be able to help with forensics to determine the true cause of death and in this instance, whether Rowdy did kill himself or someone made it look like he had, even though the handgun was next to the body.

"I just didn't feel comfortable leaving while this investigation is going on." Finn observed Rowdy's death by bowing his head. Both of us stood silently until Max shut the hearse door. "When I heard you call Betty over the dispatch this morning, I was already on my way to the office."

"I'm sorry you canceled your plans." I wanted to tell him that I was sorry he had to cancel the date, but I wasn't ready to get into how I'd erased his message. After the town found out about Rowdy Hart, I had to have at least one person on my side other than my mama. "But great intuition."

"It's no big deal." He folded his arms across his chest while both of us stood staring at the back of the hearse. "Chicago isn't going anywhere."

Max walked up with his clipboard and handed it to me with a pen for me to sign off on the release of the body from the crime scene.

"It looks like a suicide." Max's eyebrows dipped as he frowned. "But I'll do the preliminary tests to make sure."

I signed the paper and handed it back to him.

"I appreciate it." I fought for composure. I thought about Rowdy. Damn him. Did he really kill himself? Why? How was I going to tell Katy Lee and her parents?

There wasn't much left to be said. Finn and I stood in silence until we couldn't see the hearse anymore.

"Why don't you go to Rowdy's house and see if there is a note or anything there since we didn't find one here." My eyes roamed over the cemetery. I couldn't look Finn in the eyes, afraid I was going to lose control. "I'll go see the Harts and be over shortly."

"Kenni." Finn's hand ran down my arm. "I'm so sorry."

"It's fine." I bit back the tears. "It's all part of the job." I nodded and walked to the Jeep and Finn got in his car. When he was a safe distance away, I laid my head on the steering wheel and let the sadness wash over me.

The tears flowed and my heart ached. Before I could stop myself, I beat my palm on the wheel and anger took over. The fury almost choked me as I screamed out and cursed Owen, Rowdy, and Stanley. Mainly Stanley for being right about the crime rate and how it'd doubled over the past few weeks.

"I'm going to show him." My lips thinned with anger. I turned the key and started up the Jeep.

There was no time to waste. I was sure people were getting wind that someone else was dead, and I couldn't let it get to Katy Lee and her family before I told them.

They lived in a ranch home on ten acres out on Short Shun Road. They'd had a little farm with the hogs and a garden. Katy Lee was temporarily living with her parents while the new condominiums were being built out on Poplar Holler Road next to the river. She'd already put a down payment on one, but her lease on the house she was renting in town had expired, so she moved in with her parents while her new home was being built.

Rowdy had left the roost as soon as he'd graduated from high school and got his first paycheck from the city. He had a little place out in the country. His barn was bigger than the house. That was where I figured he'd been hog farming.

Whitney Hart was squatted over her flowerbed in the front of the house when I drove up. Her hair was tucked up into a big floppy straw hat that helped keep the morning sun off her exposed shoulders from the tank top and shorts she was wearing. A pair of plain gold earrings hung from her earlobes.

"Katy Lee," I heard her holler when she saw me pulling up. "Kenni Lowry is here to see you!" She yelled loud enough to go through the brick walls of the house.

I put the gearshift in park and got out.

"Kenni, you alright?" Whitney pulled the gloves off her hands, her eyes searching my face. "What's wrong?"

I tried my best to stay strong. I really did. I sucked in my chest and cleared my throat. A single tear dripped down my cheek.

"Is your husband home?" I barely got the words out of my mouth. My stomach churned. I felt nauseous.

"Kenni." Katy Lee flew out of the door. "Are you here to tell me in person about the outfit and how it made a certain someone swoon?"

She stopped when our eyes met.

"Oh God. This isn't a personal call, is it?" Her face hardened. Waverly Hart walked out of the door and stood behind Katy Lee.

"I'm sorry to inform you that I found Rowdy's body this morning." I said it hard and fast so I wouldn't hear my own words. "He..." My voice broke. "He is dead."

Waverly rushed to Whitney's side. She put her hands on her gold earrings and rubbed them before she collapsed in his arms.

"Rowdy had asked to speak to me and when he didn't show up at my office I went to the cemetery to see him. He had dug a hole." I left out the part that it looked like he'd dug his own grave, laid down, and shot himself. "He was in the hole holding the gun."

The fewer graphic details the better. They didn't need to hear all of that.

I wasn't sure if any of them heard me over their sobs. I stood there for what seemed to be an eternity, trying not to stare.

"I don't believe it." Whitney broke free from her husband's grip. She ran over to me, shaking her finger at me. "Kenni Lowry, you find out who did this, and I mean you make it your number-one priority." Her entire body trembled.

"Mrs. Hart, I'm going to do everything in my power to find out what happened to Rowdy. Max will be able to determine if it was really..." I paused.

"Suicide, Mom. That's what Kenni is trying to say." Katy Lee picked up where I couldn't. "Thank you, Kenni. What's next?"

Waverly helped Whitney into the house.

"Well, you can obviously go to Cottonwood Funeral Home to see him, but I'd give Max a few hours to prep him. I'm going to head on over to Rowdy's to see if I find any sort of note or reason why he would do this, and I'll treat it as a crime scene." I grabbed Katy Lee and wrapped her in my arms.

She was like steel. Stiff. Unemotional.

"Those earrings my mama is wearing were from Rowdy." Her voice was flat. "It was his first big purchase after he took the job with the county. He didn't make much money and Viola White had given him a deal. He was so proud and Mama loves them." She stepped away from me. "Thank you, Kenni. We will wait for your assessment."

"Oh." I looked into her eyes. They were glossed over and blank. "I'll call you soon. Tell your parents I'll be in touch."

Like a good southern woman, Katy Lee stood on the front porch and watched me get in the Jeep and drive off. From the rearview mirror, I watched as she got smaller and smaller as the distance grew between us.

"Kenni! Kenni!" Betty's shrill, excited voice trilled over the walkie-talkie. My Jeep nearly jumped into the ditch on the side of the country road.

I pushed in the button. "Go ahead, Betty."

"Is it true? Is Rowdy Hart dead?" she asked. "The dispatch is going nuts and there is a picket line outside of Cowboy's about the crime rate in Cottonwood."

"Picket line?" I asked, putting my personal feelings aside for the Hart family. No matter how I felt, I had a job to do.

"So it's true? Rowdy Hart killed himself?" She gasped between words.

"Yes," I said softly. "It appears that way. I'm on my way to his house to meet Finn and go over every square inch to find out why he'd do this."

"What do you want me to do about the picket line?" she asked.

"Nothing."

I clicked off and headed straight on over to Rowdy's house,

where Finn was waiting next to his car. He was on the phone. I was a little surprised he'd not gone in the house.

"We will definitely reschedule. I'm looking forward to it. In fact, I'm pretty pumped to see you," I heard him say off in the distance. I slammed the door so he'd look over at me. "Gotta go. Love you."

There was no time to worry about what Finn and his woman friend were talking about.

"Why haven't you gone in the house?" I asked.

"I found this on the door and thought I'd wait for you." He held up a baggie with a handwritten note inside and Rowdy's signature at the end.

The note was pretty much a confession for the murder of Owen Godbey.

He wrote that he and Owen had been working together and smoking pot after work every night. When the flowers came up missing, Owen had confessed one night when they were high that he took the flowers since they were grown by Myrna. Owen had sent the flowers off to the lab to see if they could extract the growing recipe because he was in need of money for his medicine. Rowdy also said that he got so mad about Owen stealing that out of a fit of rage—the drinking and drugs only encouraged him more—he'd put antifreeze in Owen's drink and bound him with the only thing he had, electric fencing. He'd even confessed to giving him the shock to make sure he was dead. After he sobered up, he was frantic. He knew that Myrna had fired Owen because he tried to steal her growing recipe. So he tromped through the woods, which was only about five acres away from Myrna's property, and threw Owen in the greenhouse. It was a confession detailing exactly how we'd found Owen.

"I wonder if he was going to confess to me yesterday. Stanley walked up and interrupted us." I looked at the handwriting. "That's when he told me he'd stop by, and when he didn't show..." I didn't have to recall the rest. Finn knew it.

"When I went to see him yesterday about the stolen flowers, he didn't say anything about it being Owen. In fact, he was angry that someone would do it." There was something awfully fishy about this letter. "In his letter, he says that Owen confessed. Something doesn't add up."

"Well, let's go look inside. If this is true, then we should have no problem finding all of the evidence." Finn pointed down to the metal pan just inside the door in the foyer.

It was one of those shoe tins. Next to the tin was another basket with socks in it. There was a pair of shoes in the shoe tin.

"No shoes allowed in this house and Owen was found without his shoes." Finn took out a plastic evidence bag and bagged the shoes. "Owen's?"

Chills ran down my spine. Was Rowdy really the killer?

"So Owen came over here after they worked, took his shoes off, smoked pot, got drunk, and confessed to stealing." I walked through the small house and out to the screened-in porch, where there was a small bong and a trash can with empty beer cans in it. "That simple?"

"Anything is possible," Finn stated.

"I know Rowdy. He might've been named after the wrestler Rowdy Piper, but he was a big teddy bear." I just couldn't believe that someone I'd known, or thought I'd known, all my life could do this.

"Kenni," Finn said.

I turned my head. He had a knife.

I gulped.

"How did he know I was at the tow company?" I got an evidence baggie and had Finn drop the knife inside. "There is something fishy going on."

"This looks like the exact same knife you found in your

Jeep." He looked between me and the knife. "Explain that." Finn took a step back. "Listen, I know that you are best friends with his sister and probably consider them family, but you have to look at the hard evidence."

"The hard evidence is that he smoked pot." I looked up and Finn was shaking the evidence bag with the knife.

"And he just so happens to have a knife matching the one that someone stuck in your Jeep with a threatening note?" He asked a good question.

"I'm going to grab all the cans and the bong so we can test for saliva from two people. Owen and Rowdy." I took some evidence bags out of my bag and put down markers, making the appropriate notes as I went along. "I'm not saying you're wrong. I'm just saying this looks all too convenient for me."

Finn proceeded through the rest of the house and put down markers in the spots where we thought there might be evidence of importance to the case. Rowdy Hart's house had officially become the scene of a probable killer's life.

After we scanned the house, we walked outside to get a look in the barn. The hog pens were still outside with a slop trough as well as some leftover dried-up pig feces.

"Owen did have feces on him," I noted. Finn put down a marker and took some samples as I walked inside the barn. As much as I didn't want to accept it, Rowdy Hart was beginning to look more and more guilty.

Just inside the door was a tractor along with some gardening tools and a couple cans of antifreeze, next to some rolled-up electric fence exactly like the one that was wrapped around Owen's ankles.

I snapped pictures, took samples, and made notes of everything. It all seemed to tie in.

"I guess we have the killer," Finn said after he saw the main evidence. The murder weapons used on Owen Godbey.

Finn was right. The proof was there right for anyone to see.

"Hmmm." Poppa appeared. "What are you thinking?"

"I think this is a little too obvious," I said. "And a little too convenient."

Chapter Nineteen

I sent Finn back to the office to start processing the evidence while I took the opportunity to go and let Stanley know what exactly happened to his brother. I could've called, but I wanted to see his face and maybe ask him exactly why he had it out for me.

He and Inez were sitting on the porch in their rockers. He stood up when he saw me pull up and took a couple steps toward my Jeep before I even brought it to a stop.

"Sheriff." He acknowledged me with a cold stare.

"Stanley." My eyes slid over his shoulder. "Inez."

"Hi, Kenni." Inez waved.

"Where's that mangy mutt? He better stay in your Jeep and off my property." He jerked his head, trying to look into the Wagoneer. "I don't like dogs."

I ignored him.

"Stanley, I won't take up too much of your time, but Rowdy Hart was found dead from an apparent suicide. We found a written confession where he claimed to have killed Owen at his home. There was also evidence at Rowdy's home that coincided with the way Owen was killed." I took a step back. "I'm sorry your brother was killed, even though the two of you weren't close."

"Why would you say that?" he snapped back. "He was my

only brother. Only living family member. We were plenty close. Hell," he threw his hand in the air, "he lived next door to me."

I couldn't decipher if he was telling me a big lie or the truth. I clearly remembered Inez telling me that they didn't get along. And so did Sandy. Both of them told me how Rae Lynn had hoped the cookbook would bring them together instead of apart. None of that mattered now. I had the case solved and it wasn't any of my business about their family issues.

"Kenni-bug." Poppa appeared on the porch. He pointed to the video camera strategically placed on the front porch near the door.

"I'm going to have to ask you for that video footage for evidence to close the case." I didn't know why it seemed important, but I wanted to make sure what he'd said about Owen trespassing was true. Not that Owen trespassing would have anything to do with Rowdy's rampage, but it was just something I wanted to see.

"Fine." He didn't hesitate.

I waited next to the Jeep. Poppa came over.

"It all seems like a pretty little package." Poppa chewed over the case. "It's too neat and tidy for me."

I swallowed and tried not to appear as though I was paying attention to the empty space next to me so Inez wouldn't question me.

"I mean, I never knew Owen to do anything other than drink a little too much sometimes. But drugs?" Poppa paced between the Jeep and the porch, his hands tucked in his brown uniform pants pockets.

"Here you go." Stanley walked out the front door of the house holding a small SIM chip in his hand. "It's the same footage I showed at the meeting. Clearly you see my brother look into the camera. I have no idea why he felt like he needed to sneak over. When I confronted him, he lied, of course. I accused him of wanting to make good on the deal with the big organic stores without working with us like my mom wanted."

"Greed does do strange things to people." I took the microchip. "I'll get this back to you soon." I turned to get in the Jeep and suddenly remembered I had a bone to pick with Stanley. "Stanley, can I ask you a question?"

He nodded and slid his hands in his jean pockets.

"Why are you so hell bent on getting me out of office?" It was a reasonable question to ask the man that had single-handedly put someone else on the ballot box. "And Lonnie Lemar?"

"I think it's safe to say that Lonnie did a mighty fine job under Sheriff Sims as his deputy. He did a mighty fine job as deputy under you. Then when he retired the crime rate shot up under your regime." He said it as though I was some communist leader. I certainly didn't like the tone in his voice. It was demeaning and off-putting, like Inez claimed he was with her.

"I think it's safe to say that I had nothing to do with those crimes, and in fact, I've solved them all." I wasn't going to stand there and let him put me down, even though I was taught to respect my elders.

"It doesn't matter if you solved them. What matters are the statistics that got us there and that you did nothing to prevent the crime sprees from happening." He glared.

"Oh, like I'm a damn genie or something? I'm not a psychic. I can't predict when people are going to break into jewelry stores or kill other people. Or maybe I slept through that class at the academy." The anger in my voice was crisp and direct.

"I think it's time for you to get off my property, Sheriff. Besides, I'm heading out of town on a fishing trip up to Michigan, so it's best you don't come back until I return. And I better be able to take my brother's ashes by then." Stanley turned around and walked back up to his porch. He eased down next to Inez, who was looking down into her jar of tea. His eyes were like a wave in the ocean coming toward me with each deliberate and calculated rock of his chair.

I got back into the Jeep.

"I'm going home to see Duke." I sighed.

The evidence wasn't going to change. Rowdy had confessed to the murder and the evidence was there to corroborate his suicide note.

"Good idea." Poppa sat in the passenger seat. "Sometimes it's good to take a few hours off and distance ourselves from our work. Our brains work in weird ways."

"Yeah," I muttered, getting lost into the drive back to Free Row. I had a few minutes to get home, play with Duke, get cleaned up, and head out for Euchre night. Still, I couldn't stop all the chatter in my head. Especially when it came to the Godbeys.

"Nothing will stop him from getting what he wants." Inez's words about Stanley put a chill in my bones. The kind of chill where you had to take a long hot shower to even begin to thaw.

Chapter Twenty

Finn seemed to be satisfied that we had the killer and had decided he'd go ahead and go to Chicago for a couple of days now. There was really no reason to stop him from taking a few days off. He deserved it. The quicker I could get back to the normal daily routines of being sheriff and focusing on snuffing out Stanley's campaign against me the better.

Tibbie Bell had called to say Euchre had been postponed until tomorrow night out of respect for Katy Lee. That was fine by me. I wasn't in the mood to take in all the gossip that was already swirling around about Rowdy's suicide and Owen's murder.

After a nice long run with Duke, we had a quick supper and laid in bed with the television on for white noise. My mind was all jumbled and I needed to relax.

Duke snored next to me while I stared at the ceiling with some cable love story movie playing in the background. I wanted to say I couldn't sleep because I had Finn on my mind, but he wasn't. Though he wasn't far from my thoughts, it was Owen and Rowdy who haunted me more than Poppa's ghost.

There was no sense in trying to sleep when I couldn't even shut my eyes without seeing the evidence in my head.

I just wasn't satisfied with the outcome. The fact that Rowdy Hart would kill himself was so out of character that I really wanted to make sure all the pieces of the puzzle fit before I put the murder of Owen Godbey to rest.

Owen might've wanted those samples so he could try to replicate the crop. Since he seemed to be broke and he needed his medicine so badly, then it would make sense that he'd want to grow his own crop so he could make good on the deal Rae Lynn had started with the organic store. If Stanley and Inez weren't going to help him, then he was going to do it on his own, but it would be a full year until the okra crop was even ready to harvest.

And the fact that he was stealing the flowers off the gravestones to have the stems analyzed seemed a bit extreme and out of character for even Owen. When it came to extremes and desperation, I knew anything was possible. Still, I had to be sure.

I peeled back the covers and put on my uniform. I grabbed my bag, keys, and phone.

"Come on," I called for Duke when he stood at the door giving me those big doggie eyes. "I'm just going to the office. You can come along."

"Where we headed?" Poppa appeared in the backseat of the Wagoneer when I pulled out of Free Row and headed down Main Street toward the office.

"I need to go look at the board Finn put together at the office." I stared straight ahead.

My thoughts drifted to Finn. Images of him at some fancy big-city restaurant on a date that I'd created in my head, sipping wine and looking into the woman's eyes. A smile of satisfaction from seeing him crossed her lips. I pictured her in a very skimpy dress, hair long and down her back in loose curls, sky-high heels at the end of her mile-long tan legs. Laughter popped out of her red lips before he leaned over and kissed her on the nape of the neck.

"Whoa." Poppa held onto the door when I took the quick turn to the alley behind Cowboy's. "Where did your mind just go?"

"Nowhere," I lied and put the image of the perfect date Finn was having behind me. "I want to call the lab."

After I parked the Jeep, I took out my phone and called, not even sure if anyone was going to answer.

"Tom." I was happy to hear Tom Geary answer the phone so late. He'd worked with Poppa many times and I trusted him. "It's Sheriff Lowry over in Cottonwood."

"What can I do for you, Sheriff?" Tom asked.

"I was wondering how long it would take for you to run a soil sample," I said.

"It'll take up to forty-eight hours on the fast track. Do you know what you're looking for?" he asked.

"Unfortunately I don't." I paused. It was a good question.

"Go on." Poppa encouraged me. "You can trust him. He can tell you exactly what to expect."

"I'm just not convinced that Rowdy Hart killed Owen Godbey," I said. "According to everyone I've talked to, Owen was so obsessed with the soil from his brother's okra crop that he was desperate to get the breakdown of the soil. He was stealing soil and flowers to have analyzed, apparently to try to duplicate it."

"I thought that you found a suicide note, which was good on my end because the first batch of evidence you sent over was inconclusive. Until you sent me the evidence from Mr. Hart," he said. "In fact, the main evidence was the fencing. It came back with Mr. Hart's prints on it. The antifreeze in his barn was a match as well." I could hear the shuffling of papers in the background. "I see also that the same soil sample from the hog pens matched the hog feces found on Owen. You can't get much more hard evidence than that, Sheriff."

"Right, but I don't think that Rowdy would kill Owen over flowers. And Rowdy didn't even contact me about the flowers until after Owen's death." I knew that anyone could say that Rowdy was feeling guilty for killing Owen and was trying to cover his tracks to call in a robbery, but the pieces of the puzzle weren't fitting as nicely as I liked. "I know Owen had taken some soil samples from his brother's farm. Finn contacted the lab Owen used and the results aren't back yet."

I couldn't even believe I was about to admit that I was going to get my own samples with or without Stanley's permission.

"If I bring my own samples from the same location, do you think you could get those back to me ASAP?" If there was no way he'd be able to, then there was no way I'd risk my job by trespassing. If Stanley Godbey caught me, he would definitely press charges against me and then Lonnie would get my job, election or not.

"I'm sure I could. I can't promise forty-eight hours, but pretty darn close." Tom gave me the best he could and it was good enough for me.

"Great." Now I had to make the plans to get the sample. "I'll get the sample to you soon. Do you have an after-hours drop box?" The sooner the better.

"We aren't a bank, Sheriff." Tom sounded a little offended. "But since you sound like you're in a hurry, if you have to bring it after hours and I'm not here, leave it in the empty flower pot at the back door."

"Perfect. Thank you, Tom." Poppa was right. Tom was a good man. We hung up. "It just doesn't make sense." I glanced at Poppa. "Owen was broke. He wanted the soil to grow the same okra from Rae Lynn's cookbook." I spoke slow and clear to get it clearer in my head. "If he did get the soil sample, it would take him a year to grow a new crop even if he did get the ingredients perfect. Was he going to work at the cemetery for pennies until the crop was ready to harvest? What about his arthritis? How could he work a crop?"

"Maybe he wasn't thinking that far ahead." Poppa made a good point. "What did the recipe say again?" he asked. We got out of the Jeep.

I put my key in the door of the office to let us in.

"I'll pull it out when we get inside."

I pushed the door open and flipped on the light. I held my bag tightly in my grip.

We headed over to my desk and I grabbed the composition book out of my bag. I turned to the okra recipe. I read the instructions out loud.

"It seemed like a normal recipe to me when I made them. They were good, but not kill-someone-for-the-recipe good." I stared at the words written in Rae Lynn's handwriting, hoping something, any little inkling of a thing, would jump out at me or spur any sort of spark.

Nothing. Zip. Nada.

"Then we are going to have to find out for ourselves what is in the soil." Poppa paced back and forth. "Think." Poppa walked and tapped his head. "If I were Owen and I had this book..."

"Then I would read these words very carefully." I put my finger on the page and dragged it across the words as I read out loud. "'Continue using the seeds and soil from the very first plant in the first row for each new harvest before you till the old.' And you have to till every year."

"I'm guessing it was the first plant Rae Lynn ever planted that made a good crop and she's using the seeds from that one crop to produce in all the years after." Poppa was so good about talking through things with me, which made me think more and more outside of the box.

"I need to watch the video footage," I said and turned on my laptop, where I stuck in the SIM card from Stanley Godbey.

Poppa stood behind me and watched the screen over my shoulder.

It was a typical video feed. A little grainy since it was nighttime, but the moonbeams were like a flashlight. According to Stanley, he said it was from the last few weeks.

I fast forwarded through the video to the second day since that was when Stanley told me he had seen Owen. As soon as the sun started to go down over the overgrown crop, which looked more like weeds than a real crop to me, I saw Owen tiptoeing into the view of the security camera.

"What a mess." There was a critical tone in Poppa's voice. "Rae Lynn is turning over in her grave over all the hard work she's put into the okra. That entire field but the first row is dead."

"Are you saying that because you can see her?" I snorted and kept my eyes on the screen.

"Kenni-bug, that's not funny. We work so hard on this earth to make sure the generations after us can make a good life. Rae Lynn spent years working in that field to give her family a good life, then she hands them a golden ticket by leaving them not only the recipe but a deal with a big store that wants to have her crop. They repay her by having a family feud." He touched the laptop screen with his finger. "The least they could've done was weed the darn thing."

"It looks like the crop is dead but for that one plant Rae Lynn has in the recipe." My voice faded and I sat up a little straighter when I saw the shadow enter into the picture.

Owen walked alongside the crop and bent down. The video wasn't as crisp as I would've liked it to be, but he definitely bent down and put something in a bag. This was more than likely when he'd taken the soil sample. He disappeared in between the first and second row.

"Where did he go?" My eyes darted around the screen.

Poppa bent over my shoulder. A few seconds of us watching the crop went by. A bunch of the tall weeds shuffled at the end of the row. Owen emerged with a big okra stalk in his grips. He looked around and faced the camera.

"Stanley was right." I shook my head and stared straight into Owen's eyes. "He took a stalk."

"He sure did."

Poppa straightened up.

"I bet you money he took that stalk home and replanted it in hopes he'd be able to grow his own crop." The idea percolated in my mind. "And he took it from the middle of the first row since the cookbook said to use the first row."

"Why the middle?" Poppa questioned.

"I have a sneaking suspicion Stanley watches that crop more than he leads on and he claimed he put a camera in since my break-in. My gut says something is wrong. Plus Stanley is watching the video. Why would he watch it if he didn't think he needed to? Owen probably thought if he took a stalk from the middle when it was so overgrown that Stanley wouldn't be able to eyeball it and see that there was one missing." My body stiffened. "Only Owen didn't know there was a security camera."

"Are you thinking what I'm thinking?" Poppa eased down into the chair across from me.

"That Stanley confronted Owen and killed him over the family rift? I can't help but think that Stanley did try his hand at the okra and by the looks of the video, the crop is dead. Stanley needs the recipe, which clearly tells them to use the first stalk. Also from the video, the first stalk is the only thing that looks to be healthy. And if Stanley wants to grow more crop and he too wants that organic box-store deal, then he needs that recipe just as badly as Owen needs that soil." The idea sent my pulse scurrying through my body. "You know..." I hesitated to make sure my thoughts and words came out the same. "Rowdy talked to me openly at the cemetery in front of Stanley. Stanley could've killed Rowdy and planted the evidence."

"Why on earth would Stanley want to kill his brother over something as silly as okra?" Poppa's voice was high with anxiety.

"I don't know." I looked up at the dry-erase board Finn had written all over. There was a big gap when it came to the Godbey family line he'd drawn.

In big bold print at the top he'd written the suspect list: Sandy, Myrna, Stanley, and then he'd added Rowdy.

Under "Rowdy" he wrote everything we'd learned over the past twenty-four hours about the fencing, hog feces, antifreeze, no shoes, and Owen's shoes at the scene. He'd copied the suicide note and taped it next to Rowdy's name.

Under Sandy he had written the obvious. "Ex-wife," "wanted cookbook," "best friends with Myrna," "moved," and "still friends with Owen." I picked up the marker and wrote underneath that Toots had seen Owen and Sandy at Dixon's going over the recipe the day he'd died, which was also the day they'd gone for the final divorce hearing.

Was it all too coincidental that Owen died that night? Did something go wrong when they were trying to make the recipe?

"The recipe." I froze. Sandy did have all the makings of the okra recipe on her counter when Finn and I went to her house. "Finn and I went to Sandy's and I noticed all the ingredients on her counter."

"How would she get his body back to Myrna's?" Poppa asked.

"Myrna might've helped." I'd dismissed this idea before, but now it continued to creep up on me. "Why wouldn't Stanley have killed Sandy? She knows the recipe and she was married to Owen."

"Kenni-bug," Poppa's lips tightened, "I'm stumped on this one."

I stepped back and looked at the board. Underneath Stanley's name I wrote in some information about the video.

"Do you think Sandy would've known how to use electric fencing?" Poppa asked.

"I don't know." I shrugged. "I wouldn't think so because Owen never kept hogs or even used the fencing, but you never know. I think to rule out Stanley completely, I need to get that soil sample."

We went back to the video and watched on a little faster speed. A couple of days had gone by and Owen was back at the field.

"Why would he go back?" I slowed down the video and watched Owen go straight to the first stalk of okra. The sun started to pop up over the horizon. "And at this time of day?"

Poppa and I watched. There was a bright pink twinkle that blinded the camera when the sun hit Owen just right. Right after that, we watched as he disappeared from the view.

After we watched the footage one more time, the clock on the wall read three a.m. It was pitch dark outside.

"Now would be the time to sneak out there." I already knew that Stanley would never let me get a sample unless there was a warrant, and at this hour I was sure the judge wouldn't be happy with me. "We need to see for ourselves."

"Well, standing here looking at that board is about as useful as a steering wheel on a mule." Poppa was never one for standing around when there was a crime to be solved. "Who ever heard of putting stuff up on a board and hankering over it as if a lightning bolt was going to strike some affirmation into you?" he snarled. "Let's go, girl."

Chapter Twenty-One

"There isn't anything good about this." I pulled the Wagoneer to the side of Catnip Road and shut off the lights. "I can't believe you talked me into this."

It wasn't too late to turn around, I told myself, but I knew I wasn't going to. If I was going to really get to the bottom of what my gut told me, I had to get my own soil sample and get it analyzed for myself. I had to make sure Stanley Godbey didn't kill his brother. Owen had to be desperate to use his medicine money to get a sample. The only thing I could think of that made sense was that maybe he thought if he could reproduce his mama's okra, then he'd follow through with his mama's deal with that big box organic store. Were they just being greedy? I wasn't patient enough to wait for the results. What on earth was in the soil?

"I didn't talk you into anything." Poppa poked his chest. "It's in you. Like it's in me." His eyes narrowed. "You can smell it. So can Duke."

Duke popped up between the seat when he heard his name called and tried to lick Poppa's ghost. He was right. As much as I wanted to let it go and be satisfied with Rowdy Hart's confession, I just couldn't.

The moonlight was better than any flashlight and less noticeable. I'd parked between the brothers' properties.

"This way." Poppa pointed. "Poor old Rae Lynn. I found her working in her crop when I had to tell her that Shelton had died. She collapsed right in front of my eyes."

I'd heard about that, but it was something Poppa never discussed. How the families reacted when he told them about the demise of a loved one. For a second, I wondered if Stanley was still watching the video camera, but quickly dismissed the thought since Owen was dead and Stanley didn't have any more reason to watch it so closely. Plus I had the SIM card, unless Stanley had stuck in another one.

"When you tell a family about a loved one, I think it changes you a little." Poppa was able to go through the woods with ease, but not me. I had to climb over dead logs, slog through overgrown weeds, and push back tree limbs in order to follow him to the crop. At times in the pitch dark because the woods were so thick the moon wasn't even visible.

"It's a personal thing and something I never wanted to diminish by talking about it." Everything Poppa was saying was exactly how I felt.

"Their eyes." I gulped, recalling the look on Katy Lee's face when I told her about finding Rowdy. I still needed to go to her house and check on her. As a friend, not a sheriff. "I'm not sure if I can forget the pain in their eyes."

"'The eyes are the window to the soul' is a true statement." Poppa looked back at me. When I caught up to him, I realized we were standing in the crop field.

"Wow, this is really overgrown." I looked at the tall brown stalks. "It's so overgrown the flowers haven't even budded and it just looks all dead."

The white flowers of an okra stalk were so pretty, especially in a well-kept crop field where you could see all the flowers in a row. It was almost as pretty as a picture. Like most plants, even crops, I guessed you had to have a little sunlight, and there was no way with this overgrowth that the sun could even dribble down.

"The okra crops look worse in person." Poppa noticed the camera and gestured.

"I see it." I looked up at the post Stanley had put up in the middle of the crop with the camera attached to it. "We need to hurry. Which side was the front?"

The video of Owen played in my mind, but I wasn't able to distinguish the front of the crop from the back, the first row from the last row.

"Your guess is as good as mine." Poppa shrugged.

"I'm going to have to take my chances." The tall weeds swished along my sides and my arms as I parted my way to the front of the row. At the last stalk I bent down and set my bag on the ground. I took out a baggie, put it over my hand, and dug for a scoop of soil. It was soft and easy to grab, as though it'd just been watered.

"This is strange." Poppa's eyes were as haunting as his figure. "As long as I've been living, I've never seen a crop dead in one spot but with the first stalk thriving."

"Maybe we are on to something." I stood up after I put the bag with the soil back in my bag and zipped it up.

"I've been wondering about what you said about if each one was trying to get their own deal with that store. If Stanley and Inez were keeping to Rae Lynn's deal, Owen found out about it, and bam." Poppa smacked his hand together, making me nearly jump out of my skin. His fingers formed into the shape of a gun. "Bam."

"Enough." I shushed him like someone other than me could hear him. "Let's go." I scurried back the way we came and was relieved to see the Jeep.

"Duke?" I called out when I noticed he wasn't sticking out the window. "Duke. Come," I hollered.

"Where is he?" Poppa turned and twisted.

"I don't know." I suddenly became nervous. "Duke!"

I ran around the Jeep and looked into the woods. I looked both ways down Catnip Road and didn't see him.

"Duke!" I yelled again, this time with panic settling in my gut.

"He'll be back." Poppa reminded me how Duke was accustomed to walking around Cottonwood and people picking him up.

"But he doesn't know this part of town." The desperate feeling deepened in my soul. "Duke!" Frantically I looked around. "It's not like him to leave in the night." The words hurried out of my mouth as my heart beat so fast. I felt like I wasn't able to breathe.

"Duke!" I screamed louder and louder, desperate to see him. "Duke!"

Chapter Twenty-Two

It wasn't until dawn was about to break that I decided it was time to leave Catnip Road without Duke. I had to make myself believe that he knew where he was and would find his way back or someone would find him for me like they'd always done. The only problem was that Duke didn't know the area like he knew Free Row and Main Street and the shops there.

I tried to have faith that everyone knew Duke and they'd return him.

It was too early to check with anyone that Duke was familiar with like Betty or Jolee, so I decided to turn in the soil sample I'd stolen to the lab. On the way to Clay's Ferry, I was able to talk myself into believing that Duke was safe and sound and probably either waiting on the curb of Lulu's Boutique for Jolee's truck to pull up or at the door of Cowboy's Catfish begging for a bit of tasty fried bologna.

There weren't any cars in the parking lot in front of the old brown brick building where the lab was located. The empty flower pot was next to the back door like Tom said it would be. I put the sample in there along with my business card.

My heart sank when I went back to my Wagoneer and Duke's head wasn't stuck out of the window. Why had he run off? It was so out of character for him. For a split second I wondered if the person responsible for sticking the knife in my passenger seat had taken him. But another knife just like it was found at Rowdy's, and as of this moment, his was still the only confession and all the evidence pointed to him in Owen's death. Though he didn't mention Duke in his suicide note.

The sun tugged at the horizon over the bluegrass fields on my way back into Cottonwood. I pictured Duke hanging out the window with the fresh morning wind blowing back those big floppy ears and his tongue flailing all over.

Instead of heading straight into the office, I drove by of all of Duke's favorite places to frequent, but there was no sign of the ornery pooch.

"Betty." I pushed the walkie-talkie button and talked into the speaker velcroed on my shoulder.

"Good morning, Sheriff." Betty immediately got back with me.

"Duke isn't at the office, is he?" I asked.

"Haven't seen him," she chirped. "Is he supposed to be?"

"I can't find him." There was no way I was going to tell her that I'd lost him on Catnip Road. "I think I'm going to go home and hook up to the system there." I was able to use my home computer to log into our system and finish up paperwork. "Plus, I want to be home in case Duke shows up."

"Alrighty," Betty said. "I'll keep in touch."

My day was spent worrying about Duke, looking outside a million times, and typing in the report about Rowdy. Between all of that, I talked to Max, who hadn't gotten the forensics back on the bullet and fragments, but swore it should be soon. I completed what I could on the report and saved it. And of course, Mama burned up my phone telling me all the people who had committed to put a "Re-elect Lowry" sign in their yard.

By the time I got all of that done, it was nightfall and time to head on over to Tibbie Bell's house for the rescheduled Euchre night.

I pulled up to the curb and noticed everyone had already

gotten there. I grabbed my phone, jerking the charger with it and stepping on it as soon as I got out of the Jeep.

"That's not good." My chin tucked into my chest to see exactly if it was my charger that'd I'd crunched under the heel of my cowboy boot.

It was. A loud sigh escaped me. I hoped it wasn't a foreshadow of the rest of the evening.

The regulars were at Euchre, minus Katy Lee and Jolee, which I expected. Jolee was my partner and she'd told me earlier that she was going to go sit with Katy Lee since she was taking the news about Rowdy's death and his confession hard. So it was up to Tibbie Bell to find a replacement since she was in charge of our Euchre group.

"How are you?" Tibbie's accent dragged out the "u" sound. She frowned.

"I'm alright." I glanced over her shoulder at where the Euchre tables were set up and ready with bowls of peanuts, M&M's, and a deck of cards stashed in the middle of each. There were four chairs around the table for the two pairs of teams.

"Tonight your partner is going to be Camille," she leaned in and whispered.

"Shively?" I questioned. I'd not seen Camille since I had almost stuck her in jail for killing Doc Walton. Even though I sent a note letting her know the outcome of Doc Walton's death and apologized for questioning her, I'd yet to see her around town.

I was going to have to make good with her since she was the only doctor in town now that Doc had met his maker.

Tibbie nodded. "Play nice, Kenni." Her long brown hair was straight and parted down the middle. She turned on the balls of her feet. Her hair swung like a horse's tail and nearly knocked me down.

"Kenni is here," she announced, stepping out of the way.

"The food is in there." She pointed to her dining room, where she had on display all the food the Sweet Adelines brought. "Your mama brought them brownies." She patted her thin hips. "I'm gonna have to do extra leg lifts this week." She waved me in. "Come on. You're gonna let the flies in."

I headed straight for the food since I'd spent most of the day looking for Duke and trying to stay satisfied with what little investigation I'd done in the middle of the night. I'd almost decided not to come to Euchre, but there was no sense in staying at home or going to the office only to stare down the board and work all sorts of scenarios in my head on why I believed Rowdy Hart had not killed Owen Godbey.

"Well, I'm ready." Edna Easterly moseyed up to me with her fedora perched on top of her head, notebook in one hand, and pen in the other. "What do you got? You did say I'd get first scoop."

She reminded me of the favor I'd promised when I asked her to find Sandy Godbey's address, which reminded me to ask Myrna why she took it out of my pants pocket. I cocked my head to the right and watched Myrna sipping on a tea in the corner of the room.

"Why on Earth did you print that story about Inez and Myrna?" I wanted an answer.

"It's my job. Not to mention grabbing headlines that help me sell out." There was excitement in her voice. "I'm even reprinting it in tomorrow's paper."

"Y'all talking about the catfight?" Viola White walked up with a mink stole on her neck. She rubbed it and the vintage heart-shaped charms that hung off her charm bracelet jingled. "I bought two papers. One for me and the other I sent to my friend in California." She chomped down on a piece of cauliflower she'd snatched from the veggie platter.

Edna waited until Viola walked away.

"Scoop?" She wiggled her brows.

"According to Rowdy, Owen had been stealing the flowers off the graves so he could try and get Myrna's secret growing recipe." I shrugged and grabbed a plate from the stack. I tucked a napkin in my pants pocket along with a plastic fork. "They'd been drinking, and when Owen confessed, I guess Rowdy lost his mind." I scooped up a big spoonful of Viola White's meatballs. I had heard her secret was putting grape jelly in the Crock-Pot with them. Of course, I'd yet to try that and probably never would.

"That's no scoop," Edna snarled. She stopped writing. She kept her pen on the pad and glanced up at me. "Rowdy Hart killed Owen Godbey over flowers?" Her brows cocked. Her forehead wrinkled.

I nodded and put a couple of Mama's brownies on my plate, careful not to let them touch the meatballs. Food touching gave me more heebie-jeebies than a dead body.

"Are you sure?" Edna questioned.

"Positive." I forked a meatball. I told her how Owen had died as well as where I found the evidence. "Now, you print that along with how good of a job I'm doing on the front page tomorrow."

I didn't tell her why we thought Owen had stolen the flowers.

"I will." Her lips pursed together. "But I have to say that I really thought there was something juicier to the story."

"Here you go." Mama barged her way in between me and Edna. She stuck a pin on Edna's shirt. "Now, you be sure to vote for Kenni in the election."

"Thank you, Mama." I gave her a peck on the cheek and she scampered along, putting Vote for Lowry pins on everybody she passed, including Camille Shively, who I was certain wasn't voting for Lowry.

Our eyes met. Camille gave a slight smile. Her black hair was neatly parted on the side and barely curled under, touching her collarbone. She was a nice person and everyone in town loved her. I guess she took offense when I accused her of being a murderer.

She walked over to the food table and stood in front of me.

"Kenni, how is Tiny Tina's going?" she asked about the prescription she'd given me for stress. A relaxation massage from Tiny Tina's, of all places.

"You mean the olive-oil rubdown?" I asked in a joking manner. I was sure a visit to Tiny Tina's wasn't going to cut all the stress I'd had and I was right.

"You never gave it a chance, did you?" She tsked. "You probably shouldn't be eating those meatballs because the fat content can wreak havoc on your brain along with the sugar in those brownies."

"I think I'll take my chances. I'm starving." I took the brownie and chomped down on a big bite. "Anyways, have you seen Duke?"

"I haven't. Is he okay?" she asked and picked up a plain carrot stick. The carrot snapped when she bit down.

Inwardly I groaned. What was up with the carrot stick when she had all this good food the Sweet Adelines had made?

"He's been missing since the middle of the night." Suddenly I wasn't so hungry anymore. I put the plate down on the table. Maybe later after a round of cards.

"I bet someone on Free Row put him in their house and isn't going to give him back," Mama said on a fly-by.

"I didn't lose him on Free Row." I recalled seeing Camille's name on Owen Godbey's medication. "I was at Owen's trailer, tying up loose ends," I lied. "And he was with me in the Jeep, but when I came out, he was gone."

"Doesn't he run off some?" Camille asked, her head cocked.

"He does in town, but not out there." The corner of my lips turned down. "It's also unusual that he hasn't shown up. When he does run to Jolee's truck or Cowboy's, he's only gone an hour or two. Not a full day."

"That's awful. I'll be sure to keep an eye out." She grabbed another carrot.

"Thank you. I hear we are partners tonight." I wasn't sure how to lead into asking her about Owen Godbey. "Jolee is hanging out with Katy Lee tonight."

"Ah." Camille's chin lifted into the air.

"I know that you probably won't tell me without a subpoena, but on Owen's autopsy report, it showed he was on arthritis medication and it was expensive." The words casually come out of my mouth. "Why does it cost so much?"

"He didn't have insurance." She chomped on the carrot. "I had tried to get him all sorts of coupons, but it was still expensive. He even refused to take generic drugs."

"How bad was the arthritis?" I asked.

"Pretty bad. Both knees, one hip, his left hand, and starting in the other hip."

"I'd heard he'd stopped taking the medicine because it was so expensive and he couldn't afford it," I noted.

"Afford it?" She asked. "Are you sure we are talking about the same medication?"

"No." The line between my brows deepened. "I'm talking about the medication that you prescribed. According to Sandy, his ex..."

"I know who Sandy is."

Her eyes shifted. She turned her head as though she were looking around to see if we were alone.

"Is there something you want to tell me?" I asked.

"Sandy and Owen had come to see me about the medicine about a week ago." She took a deep breath and stared at me for a few seconds. On the exhale she said, "I figure you are going to get a warrant for his records so I might as well tell you."

"Tell me what?" I was all ears.

"Sandy had heard about cannabis and how it can help with many diseases, including arthritis."

"As in pot?"

"Yes," she confirmed. "Cannabis is medical marijuana. Of course, I told them that I wasn't able to prescribe them medical marijuana because of the fact that it was illegal in the state of Kentucky. However," she paused, "if they went to say, Colorado, they could go into any cannabis store and purchase it without a prescription. Plus, it's pretty cheap."

"There you are." Toots waltzed in, her hair practically the color of flames. "I've been calling you for hours."

"You have?" I took my phone out of my pocket. "No juice." I showed her the dead phone. "I've been on it all day looking for Duke. He's missing."

"I heard, honey. Jolee came in to get ice cream and all sorts of I'm-feeling-down food to take over to Katy Lee's. She asked if he'd been in there begging for food. I kept this out all day for him." She pointed to her right eye. "It's my good eye. I can see twenty-twenty in it." She pointed to her left eye. "This eye ain't no good."

"What do you mean?" Camille asked Toots and leaned in to get a look at that left eye.

Toots started to explain all her ailments, but my mind was on smoking pot and Owen. I headed out to the Jeep and plugged in my phone. As soon as I plugged it in, my messages popped up. Sure enough, all of them were from Toots. She never said what she wanted so I went back inside.

Toots was bent, her head over the back of the chair while Camille shined a flashlight Tibbie had given her to get a look into the gimp eye.

"You come on by the office tomorrow and we will see what we can do." Camille pulled a business card from her pocket like Cottonwood was so big she needed to give me directions.

When Camille walked off, Toots turned her attention to me.

"Like I said, I tried calling you earlier." Toots popped one of Mama's brownies in her mouth. "Sandy..." she mumbled, crumbs falling out of her mouth.

"What?" I asked.

"Sandy came into Dixon's. She picked up some of Myrna's flowers from the fresh-cut section. She said that she was going to see Inez and make peace with her. The Godbeys are the only family she's got." Toots nodded.

"When was this?' I asked.

"About five hours ago." She shoved another piece of brownie in her mouth. "I called that hunk too."

"You called Finn?" I asked.

"Yes. Did you know he's in Chicago?"

She looked down the table of food to see what the next treat was going to be.

"I did. Everyone has a right to a vacation, especially since I've got everything under control." I added in that little bit for my reputation. "I do hope you get a pin from my mama. The election will be here before you know it."

"Yes." She bit on the edges of her lips. "About that..." She wagged her finger before she decided to walk away.

"What was all that about?" Tibbie walked up, shuffling a deck of cards in her hands.

"Nothing." I glanced at Camille sitting at a table and then back at Tibbie. Cannabis? Okra crops? Cookbook? The words rolled around in my head. I put my hand on Tibbie's forearm. "Say, I need to go." I gestured to the door. "I'm sorry. I'm sure you can play without me tonight."

"No, no, we can't, Kenni," Tibbie scolded me. She shifted on her cowboy boots, her hip jutted to the side. "I had to practically pull Camille's teeth to get her here."

"Yeah. Sorry," I called and hurried out of the house. My phone was chirping a message when I got in and my heart sank when I saw Max's name. Not that I wasn't happy to hear if he had some news about Rowdy's autopsy, but I was really praying it was someone who'd seen Duke.

"Sheriff, it's Max." His voice boomed through the speaker. "Owen did have marijuana in his system so that means he'd smoked it pretty close to his death." Which I already knew from Rowdy's note. "I'm ruling that the antifreeze is definitely what killed him. Also, the bullet forensics from Rowdy Hart's autopsy have come back from the lab. I hate to tell you this over voicemail, but I wanted you to know as soon as you could that it is impossible that Rowdy Hart committed suicide. He was shot from a far distance away. The bullet was built to explode in his brain as soon as it hit. The bullet shattered and all the fragments were still embedded. That's why there wasn't an exit wound." He paused. "This means you don't have the killer yet. And it also means they thought it would look like a suicide, but really aren't smart enough to realize the difference in what the wounds would look like."

I kept my hands on the steering wheel to keep them from shaking.

Camille said that Sandy and Owen had been to see her about cannabis. She also said that cannabis was cheap and it did help with arthritis. It was the perfect solution for Owen, but why kill him?

I pulled out the file from my bag and opened it. The notes about the nights Owen had crept into the okra crop jumped out at me.

"The second night was really the early morning. The pink sunspot blocked Owen's actions." I read the words I'd written on the paper. "Pink sunspot," I repeated. "The pink sunspot. Pink converse high-tops." My jaw dropped, remembering the shoes Sandy had on when Finn and I went to visit her. Sandy wanted that okra crop just as bad as Owen. "Sandy." I snapped my fingers. "That is why she was being so nice to Owen up until he was murdered. It makes perfect sense. She only wanted that recipe book out of the divorce and when she didn't get it…"

I couldn't help but believe that money and greed were what got Owen killed.

The old Wagoneer was traveling so fast, I was afraid the wheels were going to fall right off. There was no time to waste. I had to get to Inez's house as fast as I could. Especially since Toots said that Sandy was going with a bouquet of flowers to make amends. Stanley wasn't home.

"Amends my hiney." I smacked the steering wheel. My phone chirped. "Hello, Tom." I wedged the phone between my ear and shoulder.

"Sheriff, your soil sample is back. And the findings are astonishing." He started talking gibberish to me in a very excited voice. "Lignite, coco fibre, perlite, pumice, compost, peat moss, bone meal, bat guano, kelp meal, greensand, soybean meal, leonardite, k-mag, glacial rock dust, alfalfa meal, oyster shell flour, earthworm castings, and mycorrhizae."

"Huh?" I had no idea what he was talking about. "Can you speak in English?"

"Your soil sample is one of the best soils for premium buds. I mean, top-notch marijuana growing. Better than any one crop soil I've ever seen." His words made me bring the Jeep to a screeching halt.

"So are you telling me that the soil sample I brought you is from a marijuana crop, not an okra crop?"

Drugs? In Cottonwood?

Use the soil from the first stalk for next season's crop. Rae

Lynn was trying to tell them how to grow marijuana. No wonder the okra crop was practically dead. Rae Lynn left the cookbook to Owen and the crop to Stanley. Without one, the other couldn't grow the marijuana, nor make the millions off the organic store deal. But what kind of organic store sold marijuana?

Regardless, she wanted them to get along after she died, but that backfired. Sandy's words rang in my ear. Stanley couldn't grow premium weed if he didn't know the seeds he had to have, which according to the cookbook was first row, plant one. Owen needed Stanley's permission to use the soil. Rae Lynn sure was a smart one. It wasn't okra that Rae Lynn had been growing like everyone thought—it was marijuana.

"Definitely not okra." Tom Geary guffawed through the phone. "Weed. Grade-A bud. The kind you could sell in one of those shops out west."

"Like Colorado?" I questioned.

"Definitely like Colorado," he answered back.

"You mean the grower could make money off selling the crop to one of those organic weed shops?" I had to get all my facts straight.

"Definitely. There's big bucks in that industry. I mean, life-changing dollars." Tom told me everything I needed to know and more.

"Thanks, Tom." I threw the phone down on the seat and thumbed through the file again. I swear I had read something about Colorado. I flipped page after page until I came to the part about the organic store.

"What if the organic store isn't for the okra?" I asked out loud. Poppa appeared next to me. "You aren't going to believe this." I reached for my phone and dialed information. "I need a number for Can-B Organic Shop in Denver, Colorado," I said to the information operator.

Can-B. I shook my head. Instantly I knew it meant cannabis.

"Yes, please connect me," I told the operator when she asked if I wanted to pay the extra charge to be connected.

It might be nighttime here, but there was a two-hour time difference between Kentucky and Colorado.

"Mr. Wooten's office," the woman on the other end of the line answered.

"Good evening." I tried to sound as sweet as I could. "This is Sandy Godbey and I wanted to talk to Mr. Wooten."

"Mr. Wooten has said all he is going to say to you." The woman's voice was hard. "He already told you that if you didn't have the necessary paperwork, then he wasn't going to do business with you or your husband."

"I understand that," I lied as my mind rolled over the details in Rae Lynn's will. "But I do have new information about the product and the distribution."

"What type of information?" she asked.

"I'd like to discuss that with Mr. Wooten." I squeezed my eyes closed, giving good vibes through the phone.

"Hold please." Before I could say anything else, there was some elevator music blaring in the phone.

My phone chirped. I pulled it away from my ear. The battery was only at ten percent.

"Come on," I encouraged Mr. Wooten to pick up before the phone died.

"What can I do for you, Mrs. Godbey?" Mr. Wooten was a nasally fellow.

"Can you tell me one more time what paperwork it is that you need in order for me to get the okra in your store?" I asked, wanting to make sure I'd said okra just in case my hunches about the weed was wrong.

"Okra?" he questioned, a confused tone in his voice.

"Yes."

"Are you sure you meant to call me, Mrs. Godbey? Or have you been using your own product?" He snorted.

"Excuse me?" I asked.

"Listen, I'm done playing games." His voice turned serious. "The cannabis industry is a big business. Your product is one of the best I've ever tested. In fact, my arthritis has completely gone away. I'm willing to make a deal like your mother-in-law had stated, but unless you have the rights to the crop soil, then you and I are done." A deep sigh crossed the phone line. "You'd be a fool not to come to some agreement with your other family members. If you can get your brother-in-law and his wife on board and sign the papers, each of you would be instant millionaires." He paused and so did my thought process. "I'm sorry to hear about your husband."

Cannabis? Marijuana? Millionaires? Even though Poppa and I were throwing around the idea, it was now no longer just a thought. I had to be on to something. I knew it.

I jerked the Wagoneer to a stop. Everything that Tom Geary had told me was making sense.

"I'll get back with you." I clicked the off button.

Stunned, I sat there for a second. Rowdy had said that he'd smoked pot with Owen.

"What happened?" Poppa appeared next to me.

Slowly I turned my head toward him. My mouth gaped open. It closed and opened a few times, but nothing came out.

My mouth was dry. I gulped.

"It all makes sense now." I choked out the words.

"What?" Poppa asked.

"Cannabis."

The word sounded so funny coming out of my mouth. I hit the internet button on my phone and typed in "okra plant." If my hunches were right, I knew what was going on.

I pushed down on the walkie-talkie to tell Finn to meet me there, but realized he was still out of town. I was going to have to confront Sandy alone. And without Duke.

I held the wheel with one hand and grabbed the old siren off the floorboard. With my eyes glued to the road, I rolled down my window, licked the suction cup, and stuck the beacon on top of the roof. The colors twirled and swirled on the road ahead of me, lighting up the night.

The rush of it all had my adrenaline pumping. This was the chase that hooked us cops like a drug. It was the rush that was instilled in our memories and the times we lived for. These type of events might've been few and far between, but they were embedded on our soul.

At the beginning of Catnip Road, I briefly brought the Jeep to a halt and pulled in the siren. I didn't want to let them know I was there.

"Rae Lynn wasn't growing an okra crop in that first row." I showed Poppa my phone. "That is a pot plant. Those are pot leaves and they look a lot like okra leaves. That first row in Rae Lynn's crop is pot, Poppa. Marijuana."

"You mean to tell me she was growing wacky tobaccy?" Poppa's face contorted.

"And since it's illegal in Kentucky, the organic company she made a deal with is in Colorado. Rae Lynn had disguised how to grow her illegal activities in the recipe book so if anyone found the book, they wouldn't know what she was talking about."

"Huh?" Poppa asked.

"Not only that, the recipe clearly states to take the first seeds from the first row for the new crop. Owen and Stanley needed each other's inheritance to get the Can-B deal, which was going to make them millions," I continued to ramble.

It was all making sense to me.

"Huh?" Poppa asked again.

"Remember how the okra crop was practically dead the night we snuck over there?" I asked Poppa.

He nodded.

"The dead stuff was the real okra crop. But remember how the first stalk in the first row was actually growing and we commented on how the flowers had budded?" I asked and he just looked stunned. "That's the pot plant and exactly where Owen had taken the soil. Only he followed the recipe because he didn't know it was actually pot. Rae Lynn gave Owen the recipe and Stanley the land so they could keep growing the marijuana as a family business."

"What does that have to do with Sandy?" Poppa asked.

"I'm not sure, but if I had to guess, I'd say she was onto the pot-growing operation. Somehow I think she knew. She stayed all chummy with Owen up until the day of his death when he wouldn't turn over the recipe book after she lost in court." I snapped my finger. "And they'd gone to see Dr. Shively about the medical marijuana together. I can only guess that Owen found out that his soil sample was pot and since he'd been smoking with Rowdy, his arthritis was feeling better, which lead him to seek out the medical marijuana."

"Your phone call confirms that Sandy has been in contact with Can-B and Mr. Wooten," Poppa said. "Which means she knew about the operation. But did Stanley know?"

"I don't think so, because Mr. Wooten said that he needed the papers signed by Stanley and Inez." My heart nearly stopped.

I remember Inez saying something about Stanley being out of town, and if she was out there on their farm all alone and Sandy was going to take her flowers, I had a feeling Inez might be in trouble.

"Only Sandy didn't know the cookbook was actually a composition notebook." Poppa's eyes drew down to the space between us, where I had my bag with the cookbook tucked inside.

"Right," I agreed. "Owen found out about the operation and for some reason she killed him. Sandy is supposed to be with Inez right now."

Poppa grabbed the handle of the door and threw his pointer finger in front of him, pointing to the road. "Hit it. Maybe we can save Inez."

Chapter Twenty-Three

Poppa's face froze and he held on tight as the Jeep zoomed down Catnip Road.

"I hope we aren't too late." The closer we got to Stanley's driveway, the faster the Wagoneer went. "I'm scared Inez is going to be the next victim."

Poppa looked too scared to say anything. Finally, he quipped, "If you don't slow down, it will be too late."

"At this point, I wouldn't put it past Sandy to go in Inez's house, and if Inez didn't cooperate with Rae Lynn's wishes on growing the cannabis to sell out west, she'd kill her. Especially with Stanley in Michigan." I didn't pay too much attention to him talking about my driving. "I can't believe we didn't notice Sandy's pink high tops in Stanley's video."

It was the subtle and small things that helped put the pieces of Owen's and Rowdy's murders together.

If there was the slightest chance that Sandy heard my siren, I wasn't convinced she wouldn't kill Inez to keep her silent and run off. It was best if I used my senses and parked down the street, armed and ready to pounce.

"I keep wondering if Stanley knew about the crop because he stopped farming the okra right after he moved into Rae Lynn's house. Stanley wasn't going to have any part of growing marijuana. When Mr. Wooten told me on the phone to have my brother-in-law and his wife sign them, it would make sense that he didn't," I said.

"I have to say that Owen did know if he'd gone to Dr. Shively and asked about the medical marijuana. In that case, poor Rowdy was just a bystander."

"Right. Rowdy was just being a good friend to Owen by giving him a job and a shoulder to lean on. He had a little weed to smoke, which they probably did after work. Owen's lips started flapping and I bet he told Rowdy everything."

"Owen and Sandy both went into the crop. The second time Stanley thought it was only Owen, but it was really Owen and Sandy, and when the sun was coming up, the pink sparkle was where the morning sun perfectly hit her sparkly pink Converse shoes."

"Rowdy was just an innocent bystander because he was a liability to Sandy after Owen confessed to Sandy that he told Rowdy." Everything was again fitting together a little perfectly, like it had with Rowdy as the killer, but now that the ballistics came back, I was more sure than ever that Sandy Godbey had not only killed Owen, but also Rowdy.

I jerked my bag up from the floorboard and grabbed my handgun out of it.

"Don't you need to call backup?" Poppa asked.

"Who am I going to call?" I glanced over at him. "Finn is in Chicago until tomorrow and Lonnie is already putting together a campaign. I'm going to need your eyes."

"You got it, Sheriff." Poppa grinned ear to ear.

It was the first time he'd called me Sheriff.

I headed up the side of the property in the low area of the woods because my cowboy boots would be clunky on the gravel drive. I didn't want to alert Sandy I was there at all. When I got closer to the house, I could see Sandy's car was pulled up right to the front porch. The light was on.

There was a shadow that moved in one of the front windows. I unsnapped my revolver and straightened my arms with my gun in my grip and my finger on the trigger. I assessed the ways into the house. She was in the front, which would make the back a better choice to try to slip in and get my bearings about me and calculate a plan.

If Sandy had Inez in a compromising position, I'd have to go in full force. There was no way of knowing until I got inside. These were the types of situations the academy trained me for.

The adrenaline pumped in my veins with each tiptoe closer and closer to the side of the house. I put my back up against the brick and brought my hands up in the prayer position with the barrel pointing to the heavens. I was going to need all the help I could get.

I mouthed a little prayer before I stumbled over a chain and cursed under my breath, nearly knocking myself out from hitting the doghouse.

That mangy mutt better stay in your Jeep. I remembered Stanley's displeasure when I'd come to get the surveillance. If he didn't like dogs, why did he have a doghouse? I ran my hand over the roof of the doghouse and wondered if Rae Lynn kept a dog and if she did, was it to keep her pot-growing scheme protected? Or did Stanley really have a dog and didn't want Duke to find it?

Movement in the doghouse made me pause. I closed my eyes and took a deep breath. If I moved and there was a guard dog in there, then it could bark to high heaven, bite me, or worse, expose that I was out here.

I stopped. The movement stopped. A whimper echoed. I grabbed my phone and tried to turn on the flashlight, but it'd not charged enough and was dead again. Slowly I bent down and used one eye to peer in the side of the doghouse. The animal moved. It was big. It whimpered again.

My eyes adjusted to the dark and big brown eyes stared back at me.

"Duke?" I questioned. The animal jerked and shook as my eyesight adjusted completely. "Duke!"

I pushed myself inside the doghouse and noticed he was chained up and muzzled. There was a padlock on the heavy chain. I unbuckled the muzzle and opened myself up for slobbery kisses all over my face.

"Who did this to you?" I jerked the keys from my belt and used the bump key to get the lock off. Anger swelled up in me. It took everything I had not to rush into that house, guns blazing. "You're safe now."

Both of us stopped when I heard footsteps. Heavy footsteps. Then yelling.

"I told you that this was not going down the way it was supposed to." Sandy's words were bitter. "You had to go and steal the damn dog when you knew damn good and well that I'd already stuck one of the knives in the seat of her cop car."

"Shhhh," I whispered in Duke's ear, remembering the training Finn had tried to do with him out of boredom at the office. The longer he stood there, the more treats he got.

It was that little game Finn had taught him, only I didn't have treats.

"Shut up." Stanley Godbey's voice caught me off guard. I thought he was supposed to be in Michigan on a fishing trip. "No wonder my brother was going to dump you. You yammer on and on when I need to think."

"I'm telling you that your little idea of this staying quiet is all going downhill and the smear campaign you have against that nosy sheriff isn't working. So you better figure this out, because I'm not going from one loser brother to another only to be thrown in jail because I was an accessory to murder," Sandy threatened.

"You listen to me. If it weren't for me, you'd be slumming it," Stanley threatened back.

"If it weren't for me, you wouldn't have the cookbook," she said.

"You don't have the cookbook. Your sister couldn't even keep Owen's truck long enough to go through it. That dumb sheriff has it," he said.

"Simone did the best she could. She wasn't about to let our tow company go under when you were only willing to give her a two-percent cut. Plus, that sheriff had a warrant," Sandy said.

Our tow company? I tried to think with Duke's hot breath in my face waiting for me to give him a treat. S&S Towing had to stand for Simone and Sandy. That was how the truck got towed so fast.

"All of that is under the bridge." Sandy's voice turned sweeter than a baby cooing. "Little Miss Sheriff thinks Rowdy killed Owen. She's got no clue what is going on. Besides, I talked to Mr. Wooten and he said as long as I had Owen's part, then we were good to go. Then you and I can move, get out of this hick town, and start our life rich in Colorado, baby."

My eyes nearly popped out of my head when I heard her call Stanley "baby."

The sound of smacking lips made my stomach hurt. The last thing I wanted to hear was the two of them making out. It wasn't like I could ambush the both of them. There were two of them and one of me.

I'd have to wait it out until either of them was alone. They obviously hadn't fed Duke or even cared about him. I could tell that by the way they'd muzzled him and chained him up in the doghouse, probably leaving him to die.

"Now, you go in there and you get her to sign over those papers before I knock her off the face of the Earth before we need to," Sandy threatened Stanley.

"She needs to calm down," Stanley said. "She's having a hard time believing we did this to her."

"I don't care what she believes. Get her to sign over that crop. I could just kill your mama if she weren't already six feet under."

"Don't you dare talk about the dead or my mama that way. Don't you know they will haunt you?" The anger I'd heard in Stanley's voice before was there again.

"Don't you know that she knew me and you were having an affair? That's why she set up the will like this. She left this crop to you *and* Inez. I knew I should've gone to the sheriff the day I discovered her smoking her own pot." Sandy spoke with a confidence I was sure Stanley didn't like in a woman.

"I'm glad you didn't because it was your brains, baby, that got her to thinking about making big money and here we are. That's what I'm trying to tell you," he whined. "We're almost at the finish line. I can taste it."

"The finish line is after you go in there and kill her. I'll forge her signature and then we are out of here." A few more lip-smacking noises later, the two of them stalked off into the house.

"They got Inez all tied up at the kitchen table." Poppa appeared, out of breath. Duke jumped up, forgetting about the "Shhh" game, and bounced out of the doghouse when he saw Poppa. "We've got to get a game plan."

"The game plan is this," I whispered. "You've got to get in there and tell me where Sandy and Stanley are so I can get Inez out of there."

Poppa nodded.

"You are doing good, Kenni-bug." He smiled before he ghosted off.

I was sure he was only trying to keep me encouraged by giving me a boost of confidence, but it helped.

"Okay, Duke." I took my cell out of my pocket and tried to turn it on again. Nothing. "It looks like you are my backup."

We crawled out of the doghouse. With my gun pointing down to the ground, I slid along the side of the house. I looked back at Duke.

"Shhhh." I played the game again and he sat, watching me. I poked my head around the corner of the house and looked into the backyard. The coast was clear. The closer I could get to the back kitchen door, the quicker I could get Inez out when Poppa gave me the go ahead.

"Kenni." Poppa appeared behind me and I jumped.

"Don't do that while I'm already on high alert." I sighed deeply. "Don't you have like a ghost bell or something to ring? Because I know hearing footsteps is out of the question for a ghost."

"No, I don't have a bell. Do you want to know where Stanley and Sandy are or not?" he asked.

"Of course." My head bobbled side to side to make sure we were still alone.

"They went into the basement. It looks like they are getting some digging tools. You better hurry." He ghosted away.

I ran up to the door and looked in. Inez was sitting in a chair with her back to the door. Her feet were tied on the front legs of the chair and her hands behind her.

When I opened the door, she shuffled, the chair legs knocking back and forth on the floor. I noticed a similar metal tray with shoes in it by the door like I'd seen at Rowdy Hart's house, along with a basket of socks. My eyes slid to Inez's feet—they were bare.

"Stop moving. They'll hear you," I whispered and, with arms straight out, cleared the room and walked over to her. "Let's get you out of here."

I got down on one knee next to her and placed my gun on

the floor. Quickly I untied her hands behind her. She pulled out the gag as soon as I got her legs untied.

"Help!" she screamed. "Stanley!"

"Stop it," I shushed her and grabbed my gun. "They're going to hear you."

"Help, Stanley!" she screamed louder.

I grabbed her elbow to drag her out of the house, footsteps clomping up the basement steps. As soon as I got her to the kitchen door, I gave it a swift kick and threw her out before I heard the basement door bust open.

"Hold it right there." Stanley's voice was stern and hard. "I swear I'll shoot her."

The sobs behind me made me pause and I turned around. Stanley had Sandy in his grips with a gun stuck to her head.

"You are never going to get away with this." I knew I had to come up with some fast talking to get me out of there. I put a hand behind me when I heard Inez walking back up. "You stay back."

"So far I haven't done so bad." He jerked his gun to the right a couple of times. "Put your gun down now and Inez will come in and get it."

There we stood. Me and Stanley Godbey in a standoff. I eyed Sandy to see if I could get a clear shot at Stanley's hand, but she was shaking so much that it was making his hand shake. It wasn't a risk I was going to be able to take.

"Go ahead. Shoot and kill her." His grip tightened around Sandy and when he jerked her to him, she winced. "This little hussy really played me. Didn't you?" he asked through gritted teeth.

"No." There was desperation in her voice. Her eyes bulged and she shook her head. "I love you, Stanley."

"Love him?" Inez scoffed from behind me. "He loves me."

"This is something I didn't see coming." Poppa stood

between me and Stanley. "I'm a little confused about what is going on here."

"It looks like we are in a little love triangle." I glared, my gun still pointed at Stanley.

"It's nothing like that." Stanley's eyes looked past my shoulder. "I love my wife. This," he jerked Sandy's arm up and she cried out in pain, "was a little fling to get my hands on that cookbook, but when she couldn't produce, she became a liability. But today she was a good little girl and signed Owen's name on the paper that gives me his half so Inez and I can go make a better life for ourselves just like Mama wanted."

"You liar." Sandy found her voice. "If that was the case and Inez knew it was all in the game plan to get rid of me, why did she come and threaten me to stay away the other day?"

"So you," I said to Inez, "stole Sandy's address from my police bag after Lulu gave it to you to give to me after the stained-glass party." The pieces of the puzzle were fitting together. If only I'd figured this out before now, I'd be in much better shape.

"You what?" Stanley spat.

"Go on. Tell him what you told me." Sandy was trying to pit Stanley and Inez against each other. Inez stood silent for a moment. "Fine. I'll tell him how you came to me to make our own deal and knock him out of it," Sandy said.

"Baby, I love you. You know that." Inez's voice cracked as she talked to Stanley.

"You love him so much you wanted to keep me playing along with him and then us take the crop and run." Sandy winced as Stanley pushed the gun against her temple.

"I oughta kill both of you. I'm holding all the cards now." He turned his eyes back to me. "I swear I'll shoot her and won't care. After I shoot her, I'll kill you and make it look like a murder suicide," he snarled.

I didn't move from my stance. I was going to wait for the shot. I knew Inez didn't have a gun and she wasn't moving. Sandy had closed her eyes and clenched her jaw.

"You know," I stalled for time, "it wasn't until I took the soil sample for myself that I knew what was really going on. But it wasn't until this instant that I thought you were in on it. You think you are so smart." My eyes narrowed.

"I am smart. My mama screwed me. I took care of her all these years and my no-good brother gets part of the fortune she and I were building." He adjusted his grip on Sandy. She squealed.

"But you were sleeping with Sandy." I recalled what they'd said outside.

"You what?" Inez spat from behind me. "You said you were just wooing her."

"She's lying, baby. She just wants to throw you off our plan." Stanley's lips were stiff from the anger spilling out of him.

"If wooing means he was laying down with me in my bed, well, I guess you could call it that," Sandy said. "Owen found out and that's why we got divorced. He and I were going to figure out the soil ingredients and grow our own crop for Mr. Wooten. Then he got a little crazy."

Stanley let go of Sandy and back-handed her, letting her fall to the ground. She held her jaw, blood dripping from her mouth. He planted his foot on her head.

"I told you to shut up." He pointed the gun at her head.

Duke darted through the door and jumped over me, knocking Stanley to the ground. A shot rang out and right before my eyes, Duke landed on the ground, motionless.

"Duke!" I screamed and looked down at my dog.

"Hold it right there," a familiar voice rang out from behind me. "The jig is up, Stanley." Finn walked up next to me. "Put the gun down."

Stanley looked between me and the dog. "It's just a mangy mutt." He threw the gun next to Duke's head.

Chapter Twenty-Four

I couldn't stop my legs from bouncing up and down as I sat in the waiting room of the Cottonwood Veterinarian clinic.

"Finn, how did you know I was there?" I wrung my hands.

"Toots called to tell me about Sandy, plus Tom Geary from the lab called. He told me about you taking a soil sample and I put two and two together and figured Sandy must be involved. I tried calling your phone, but it went to voicemail and Betty must've gotten her ears mixed up again because she couldn't understand a word I said. So I hurried back." He placed his masculine hand on my knee. Momentarily it stopped from bouncing. "He's going to be okay."

I bit my lip and tried to stop the tears, but it didn't help. They flowed.

"There you are." Mama and Daddy bolted through the door. "We came as soon as we heard."

Soon after they came in the door, the entire waiting room was filled with friends and Sweet Adelines. They'd transformed the counter into a food buffet.

"If y'all want some good fried green tomatoes, Jolee is frying them up outside in honor of Duke." She pointed to the On The Run truck parked in the parking lot.

"I've got plenty of coffee." Ben Harrison walked in with carafes of coffee. He and Jolee looked at each other. They gave a simple nod that put a truce between them, for the time being at least.

My heart was bubbling over. This was what I loved about a small town. No matter how far apart in views each of us were, we all came together in a time of need. They loved Duke. He was as much their pooch as mine.

"How was your trip?" I asked Finn.

"It was good. I got what I needed to accomplished." His lips curled into a smile. He left it at that and I let him. I didn't care to know the details.

It seemed like I waited for an eternity. Poppa would come out and give me updates about the surgery. The bullet had lodged in one of his ribs, next to his heart, and it wasn't clear if it was too close to the heart to get out. There was some bleeding.

Lulu had brought over a Derby Pie and served it.

"Thank you." Katy Lee squatted down between my legs. She looked between me and Finn. "I knew Rowdy didn't kill himself."

"Kenni figured it all out." He gave me the credit.

"We figured it out." I forced a smile. "We are the sheriff's department, partner."

"That's right." Mama opened her big pocketbook and pulled out "Vote for Lowry" pins, pinning them on the people who'd gathered to check on Duke. Even if they already had gotten one from her earlier in the week, she gave them another one. "One for each outfit."

I looked at Finn.

"Good job, Lowry." He nodded. "I still can't believe Stanley was going to kill Sandy once she signed off on the paperwork for the cannabis store, leaving him and Inez the fortune."

"I'm so shocked Rae Lynn was growing marijuana," I said.

"Wally Lamb showed up at the office when I took them down to the cell to wait for the state police to pick them up. He said that Rae Lynn had come to him about the crop because she'd heard it would help Owen with his terrible arthritis that he'd had since his late twenties and she hated to see him suffer. Stanley didn't want anything to do with it being grown and Owen didn't know about it. They thought their mama had gone crazy or smoked too much weed. Sandy had dropped by unexpectedly one night when Rae Lynn was sampling her pot and Rae Lynn told Sandy about medicinal marijuana and how Owen might be able to use if for his arthritis. Rae Lynn had asked Sandy to keep it secret until she researched it more. Rae Lynn had sent off a sample to Mr. Wooten and then made the deal with the Can-B store herself. She had Wally draw up the paperwork. She left Owen the recipe book that specifically told him to use the soil from the first row which was the grade-A soil she'd cultivated for the best marijuana. She gave Stanley the land. She figured once they heard about the deal and how one needed the other and the secrets that each one held it was going to bring the boys together. The affair between Sandy and Stanley was just a sidebar, but Stanley built on that after he researched the money to be made. He knew he had to have the cookbook because even though it didn't have any real value, once they presented it to Wally along with Inez's signature, Wally would be able to seal the deal with Can-B, making the Godbeys millions."

"Why didn't Wally come forward when he knew we were looking at Myrna?" I shook my head.

"He claimed it was client confidentiality." Finn shrugged. "If Stanley and Inez had skipped town and we subpoenaed him and his records, then he'd have come forward."

"Was I right on most of the puzzle?" I asked, because I'd refused to leave Duke's side.

On Finn's way over to the Godbeys', he wasn't sure what was going on, so he had called an ambulance to meet him there.

Luckily, they took Duke to the animal hospital with me in there with him.

"Sandy kept Owen close to her side until the ruling that she didn't get the recipe in the divorce and that's when she let Owen in on the secret about the medicinal marijuana. That's why they went to see Dr. Shively. Owen didn't believe Sandy at first, but he did admit that he'd been smoking pot with Rowdy and was feeling better. That's when he also snuck in to get the soil sample because he couldn't believe his mom was growing dope." Finn took a deep breath and continued telling the details. "Stanley knew about it and he started making deals on the side with Inez and Sandy, even sleeping with Sandy for her to fall in love with him. The plan to kill Owen was hatched between Inez and Stanley. When Sandy showed up at the house tonight, she was going to make her own deal with Inez, but she saw that Stanley was in town and had lied to her. From there tonight just spiraled."

I smacked my hands together.

"When I walked into the kitchen to free Inez, I noticed they had their shoes off at the door in the same kind of metal tray that was at Rowdy's house. No doubt they had planted the tray at his house."

"Right. Owen had come over to Stanley's to talk about Rae Lynn's wishes upon Inez's request. She said she told him they'd come to an agreement. It was then that Inez gave him the poison in his drink and tied him up with the barbwire Stanley had stuck in the basement from their hog-raising days. They didn't even look at his feet to realize they'd left his shoes at their house. They threw him in Myrna's greenhouse."

"You have a lot of information." I was impressed with Finn's skills so early after the arrest.

"Inez vomited the information. Begging for a lesser charge." He rolled his eyes. "Of course, I told her we'd see what we could do based on the information she had and depending on her cooperation."

"How did Rowdy play into it?" I asked.

"Wrong place, wrong time." He continued, "Inez said that Stanley had come home and said you'd stopped by the cemetery and Rowdy said something about needing to talk to you. He also had told Stanley that Owen was talking out of his head about some marijuana-growing scheme. When Stanley left the cemetery, he grabbed the antifreeze and fencing along with the knife matching the one Sandy's sister had stuck in your Jeep when you left it at S&S Auto Salvage overnight. They only wanted to scare you about Duke until Stanley saw you on the live feed on the camera. He went looking for your car and took Duke."

"I had thought about that feed, but I figured since Owen was done stealing, he wasn't watching it so closely." I gulped. "It was like everything was going downhill for Stanley and he was just going to kill anyone in his way, including my Duke." Tears filled my eyes.

"He was willing to kill anyone up until the crop was finished growing, because the crop he needs for Can-B isn't fully grown. He has another couple of weeks. He figured out by Owen coming to the first plant in the first row that that was the secret to the cookbook. Only he wanted the cookbook to see for himself. They all thought it was an actual book, not a composition notebook, because Rae Lynn never let the boys see it. That's why the real okra crop is dead and Stanley could never grow the okra."

I was in shock and awe listening to Finn.

"He went back to the cemetery and shot Rowdy from far away. Rowdy was preparing a grave and fell in and he left him there. Stanley tossed Rowdy's gun in there and Inez went to Rowdy's house and planted a suicide note. Here we are." He threw his hands in the air. "I'm so glad Toots called me."

"I'm sorry I interrupted your date." I looked down at my fingers and they fiddled with each other.

"Kenni." Finn put his hand on my leg again. "You didn't interrupt anything." His brows furrowed.

"Sheriff." The veterinarian came through the door and into the waiting room.

I jumped up, as did everyone else in the room. The silence was eerie.

"Duke is going to be just fine." His words were greeted with roars of cheers and claps. I felt like I'd just been given the world.

Chapter Twenty-Five

Duke came home from the hospital the next day and I took off a week of work. Finn said that he was more than happy to hold down the fort if there was any more crime. I prayed there wouldn't be, but still put Poppa on patrol to keep an eye out.

Duke needed me and I was going to be there for him.

"You and me, buddy." I rubbed his head lying on my pillow. I'd made him a bed out in the family room and the kitchen, but he only wanted to lay in my bed. "I know you jumped that mean man to save me."

Finn had called earlier and asked if he could come see the patient and update me on what was going on with the case. Since it had to do with illegal drugs, the Central Kentucky Drug Taskforce had come in to take over. They disposed of the crop on Stanley's property along with Owen's feeble attempt to grow his own crop from the stalk Poppa and I had seen him steal that night on the video.

The doorbell rang.

"Your friend is here." I dragged myself out of bed. I didn't bother looking at myself in the mirror. Finn Vincent wasn't interested in me. He had his girl back in Chicago.

I shuffled down the hall and opened the front door.

Finn stood on the other side with a big bright smile on his face and a pizza box in one hand, a six-pack of beer in the other.

"Straight from Chicago." He held them up. The dark-haired woman I'd seen in his wallet, who he'd told me was his sister, stood next to him. "Both of them."

"Huh?"

"Evelyn Vincent," the sultry voice greeted me. She held on to a cat carrier. "Finn has been driving me nuts to get you a Chicago pizza, and when he came up a week ago, he had forgotten it on my counter when he'd heard you were in trouble."

"Can we come in? Or I guess we can eat it out here." Finn balanced the box and beer with one hand while he ran the other through his hair. "Please, Cozmo is hungry."

"Where are my manners?" I ran my hands down my hair, instantly caring what I looked like. "Please, come in."

Both of them stepped into the house.

"Cozmo, as in Sandy Godbey's cat?" I asked and bent down to look inside.

The cat's green eyes sparkled from the back corner of the cage where the scared feline was trying to find a safe haven.

"I asked Sandy after her booking if she had anyone to take Cozmo and she said that she'd let the cat out of the house and wasn't planning on going back. Can you believe that?" He shook his head.

"I told Finn that he should also throw animal cruelty into her file." Evelyn brought the cage up to her face. "I'm going to take this baby back home with me," Evelyn said to Cozmo.

Cozmo let out a faint meow.

"Make yourself at home while I get the patient ready for company," I called, heading down the hall, a big grin on my face.

"Duke," I rushed over to the bed and whispered, "that woman whose message I erased on his machine was his sister. And she likes animals."

Both of these attributes of Evelyn were pluses with me.

I picked up the clothes Katy Lee had given me that were wadded up in the corner of the bedroom and put them on. They were a little wrinkled, but available and new. I ran a brush down my honey hair and added a little lipstick.

"You ready for company?" I asked Duke before I hurried back down the hall.

Finn and Evelyn were sitting at the kitchen table each with a beer in their hand. Cozmo was curled up in Evelyn's lap.

"Sheriff, this is Evelyn." Finn stood up like a gentleman and properly introduced her to me.

"Kenni." I bent down and gave her a hug. She was a little stiff, but that was how we greeted friends around here.

"This is where he's getting those new manners." She giggled when I pulled back.

"Excuse me?" I asked, a little confused. Finn grabbed me a beer and handed it to me with the top already popped off.

"That." Her brows lifted. There was definitely a resemblance between the siblings. Her skin was smooth and her infectious laugh added to her appeal. "When he came home, he greeted all of us with a big hug and couldn't stop talking about your charming town which is rubbing off on him. He even said 'y'all.'"

"You did?" A big grin crossed my face. I couldn't stop it.

His lip twitched up in the corner before leading into a full smile, exposing those beautiful pearly whites.

"He's told me all about your sayings." She looked at her brother with admiration.

"The sayings." My memory recalled the phone call he'd had a week or so ago when I thought he was making fun of us.

"I don't think I've ever seen him so happy." She reached over and patted him on the back.

"Enough." He stood up. "Let's go see Duke."

"Alright."

I motioned for them to walk with me down the hall.

Duke was asleep and snoring on the bed when we walked in the bedroom. All three of us looked between each other and smiled.

"Oh, let him sleep," Evelyn suggested. "He needs to heal. I'm sure I'll meet him again."

Finn grabbed the pizza box off the counter when we walked by into the kitchen. He threw it on the table and opened the cardboard lid. "This is the real Chicago pizza I told you about."

I peeked inside and saw all the meats and veggies piled high with melted cheese and thick crust.

"What kind of look is that?" he asked. I didn't realize I gave a look. "I've tried all your gravy, biscuits, hot browns, and pies. Now it's your turn." He slapped a piece of the thick greasy pizza on a napkin and pushed it toward me.

Evelyn didn't waste any time. She grabbed a piece and ate it right away. She gave Cozmo a little piece of cheese when he stuck his nose up in the air. We exchanged stories about Finn for about an hour before the doorbell rang.

"Katy Lee." I was surprised to see my friend at the door. "Come in."

"I can't." She pointed over my shoulder. "I'm here to pick up Evelyn. She might start selling Shabby Trends in Chicago so I'm taking her to look at the clothing line and then we are headed over to Ben's to taste your mama's sweet potato cakes."

"Oh." I was taken aback. "When did you meet Evelyn?"

"When Finn brought her to On The Run this morning. You ready?" she asked Evelyn.

"I am. I can't wait to taste sweet potato cakes. But I want to say bye to Duke." Evelyn walked back with Katy Lee to see Duke, who I was sure gave them his big droopy eyes for more loving.

"Didn't your mama tell you that she won the cook-off?" Katy Lee asked on her way down the hall.

"She never mentioned it." I was shocked since Mama seemed to tell me everything, even when I didn't want to know it.

I couldn't wait to ask her about it. I thought she'd been so wrapped up in the election and making posters and pins that she'd not had any room left for other things. I was wrong. Apparently, Mama had gone to cooking.

"He looks so good," Katy Lee said when she came back. She looked at Finn and grinned.

"What?" I asked between them.

"What?" Finn asked back.

"Nothing." Evelyn rushed Katy Lee out the door with Cozmo and his cage in her arms. They shut it behind them.

I looked out the front family-room window next to the door and they were already in Katy Lee's car.

"That was weird." I turned around and came nose to nose with Finn.

"Was it?" he asked. His cologne smelled so good, it made me weak in the knees.

"Uh huh." I slowly nodded my head.

"My heart was stopped for the five-hour drive it took me to get here after I couldn't get a hold of you." I could feel his breath on my cheek. "You nearly gave me a heart attack. You and I are a team."

My eyes watched as he licked his lips. I couldn't help but wonder if they tasted as good as he smelled.

I cleared my throat to make sure I was not dreaming.

He curled his hand around to my back and rested it around me. He pulled me close to him. His lips brushed up against mine. They were soft and longing.

I closed my eyes as the kiss deepened. My mind was swirling with excitement.

There was a knock at the door. Both of us took a step back.

His smile went up to his eyes.

"What did you forget?" I jerked the door open, sure it was Katy Lee.

"We are walking the streets to get the word out that Lonnie Lemar is running for Sheriff and we'd appreciate your support." Someone with a "Lonnie for Sheriff" shirt stood at the door. She had no idea who I was.

I slammed the door in her face and turned to face Finn and Poppa, who had suddenly appeared.

"I knew I couldn't leave you alone with him for one minute," Poppa scolded.

"Want another drink?" I asked Finn, knowing Poppa wasn't going to go away so Finn and I could pick up where we left off.

"Sure." Finn followed me back to the kitchen.

"I'm going to check on Duke first." I made a quick turn to go down the hallway.

"I'll go with you." Finn followed me back.

Duke lifted his head and let out a satisfying groan after Finn sat on one side of the bed and I sat on the other, both of us stroking my pooch.

Our hands touched. Our eyes met. He smiled. I knew I was a goner.

TONYA KAPPES

Tonya has written over 20 novels and 4 novellas, all of which have graced numerous bestseller lists including *USA Today*. Best known for stories charged with emotion and humor, and filled with flawed characters, her novels have garnered reader praise and glowing critical reviews. She lives with her husband, three teenage boys, two very spoiled schnauzers and one ex-stray cat in Kentucky.

**The Kenni Lowry Mystery Series
by Tonya Kappes**

FIXIN' TO DIE (#1)
SOUTHERN FRIED (#2)

Henery Press Mystery Books

And finally, before you go...
Here are a few other mysteries
you might enjoy:

PUMPKINS IN PARADISE

Kathi Daley

A Tj Jensen Mystery (#1)

Between volunteering for the annual pumpkin festival and coaching her girls to the state soccer finals, high school teacher Tj Jensen finds her good friend Zachary Collins dead in his favorite chair.

When the handsome new deputy closes the case without so much as a "why" or "how," Tj turns her attention from chili cook-offs and pumpkin carving to complex puzzles, prophetic riddles, and a decades-old secret she seems destined to unravel.

Available at booksellers nationwide and online

Visit www.henerypress.com for details

MACDEATH

Cindy Brown

An Ivy Meadows Mystery (#1)

Like every actor, Ivy Meadows knows that *Macbeth* is cursed. But she's finally scored her big break, cast as an acrobatic witch in a circus-themed production of *Macbeth* in Phoenix, Arizona. And though it may not be Broadway, nothing can dampen her enthusiasm—not her flying cauldron, too-tight leotard, or carrot-wielding dictator of a director.

But when one of the cast dies on opening night, Ivy is sure the seeming accident is "murder most foul" and that she's the perfect person to solve the crime (after all, she does work part-time in her uncle's detective agency). Undeterred by a poisoned Big Gulp, the threat of being blackballed, and the suddenly too-real curse, Ivy pursues the truth at the risk of her hard-won career—and her life.

Available at booksellers nationwide and online

Visit www.henerypress.com for details

THE DEEP END

Julie Mulhern

The Country Club Murders (#1)

Swimming into the lifeless body of her husband's mistress tends to ruin a woman's day, but becoming a murder suspect can ruin her whole life.

It's 1974 and Ellison Russell's life revolves around her daughter and her art. She's long since stopped caring about her cheating husband, Henry, and the women with whom he entertains himself. That is, until she becomes a suspect in Madeline Harper's death. The murder forces Ellison to confront her husband's proclivities and his crimes—kinky sex, petty cruelties and blackmail.

As the body count approaches par on the seventh hole, Ellison knows she has to catch a killer. But with an interfering mother, an adoring father, a teenage daughter, and a cadre of well-meaning friends demanding her attention, can Ellison find the killer before he finds her?

Available at booksellers nationwide and online

Visit www.henerypress.com for details